# Harry and the Kidnappers

## Dr. Robert A. Ernst

### Illustrated by Rose E. Grier Evans

*Dr. Bob's Tales: Book 4*

Discoveries Publishing, LLC
Palm Coast, Florida

Book design by Sagaponack Books & Design

ISBNs:
978-1-7377805-1-9 (softcover)
978-1-7377805-2-6 (hardcover)
978-1-7377805-3-3 (e-book)

Library of Congress Catalog Card Number: 2022920343

Summary: Sheriff Harry and the deputies are pulling together to save the kidnap victims and solve the mystery of the pond drying up. Professor Ludwig's latest gadgets may save the day. Rolf and his wolf pack are at their nastiest.

JUV001010 Juvenile Fiction / Action & Adventure / Survival Stories
JUV045000 Juvenile Fiction / Readers / Chapter Books
JUV039060 Juvenile Fiction / Social Themes / Friendship
JUV039220 Juvenile Fiction / Social Themes / Values & Virtues
JUV036020 Juvenile Fiction / Technology / Inventions

**www.DrBobsTales.com**

First Edition
Printed in the USA

*For Ann, always*

# CONTENTS

List of Characters . . . . . . . . . . . . . . . . . . . vii

Map of Pondville . . . . . . . . . . . . . . . . . . x

Chapter 1 . . . . . . . . . . . . . . . . . . . . . 1

Chapter 2 . . . . . . . . . . . . . . . . . . . . 11

Chapter 3 . . . . . . . . . . . . . . . . . . . . 17

Chapter 4 . . . . . . . . . . . . . . . . . . . . 23

Chapter 5 . . . . . . . . . . . . . . . . . . . . 32

Chapter 6 . . . . . . . . . . . . . . . . . . . . 40

Chapter 7 . . . . . . . . . . . . . . . . . . . . 48

Chapter 8 . . . . . . . . . . . . . . . . . . . . 55

Chapter 9 . . . . . . . . . . . . . . . . . . . . 63

Chapter 10 . . . . . . . . . . . . . . . . . . . . 69

Chapter 11 . . . . . . . . . . . . . . . . . . . . 76

Chapter 12 . . . . . . . . . . . . . . . . . . . . 89

Chapter 13 . . . . . . . . . . . . . . . . . . . . 95

Chapter 14 . . . . . . . . . . . . . . . . . . . . 104

Chapter 15 . . . . . . . . . . . . . . . . . . . . 111

Chapter 16 . . . . . . . . . . . . . . . . . . . . 124

Chapter 17 . . . . . . . . . . . . . . . . . . . . 134

Chapter 18 . . . . . . . . . . . . . . . . . . . . 140

Chapter 19 . . . . . . . . . . . . . . . . . . . . 148

About Dr. Bob's Tales . . . . . . . . . . . . . . . 156

Discussion Guide . . . . . . . . . . . . . . . . . 158

About the Pond . . . . . . . . . . . . . . . . . 160

Acknowledgments . . . . . . . . . . . . . . . . . 161

About the Illustrator . . . . . . . . . . . . . . . 162

About the Author . . . . . . . . . . . . . . . . 163

## CHARACTERS IN ORDER OF APPEARANCE

*Percy*, a turtle:
Mayor of Pondville

*Harry*, a frog:
Sheriff of Pondville

*Wreck*, a car:
Sheriff's car

*Jake*, a raccoon:
A deputy sheriff of Pondville

*Clinger*, a raccoon:
A deputy sheriff of Pondville

*Arthur*, a wolf:
Chief Deputy Sheriff of Lankasville

*Kim*, a deer:
A chief deputy sheriff of Pondville

*Bart*, a bear:
A chief deputy sheriff of Pondville

*Rolf*, a wolf:
Leader of the wolf pack

*Joey, Blackie, Thor, and Brownie*, wolves:
The wolf pack

*Stinky*, a skunk:
A deputy sheriff of Pondville

*Earl*, a crow:
A deputy sheriff of Pondville

*Ludwig*, a turtle:
Professor and inventor

*Sally*, a frog:
Pondville's event chairperson

*Red*, an ant:
General of the ant army

*Tilly*, a bear:
Apprentice to Ludwig

*Charlie*, a frog:
Mechanic and builder

*Carl*, an eagle:
Captain of the eagle squadron

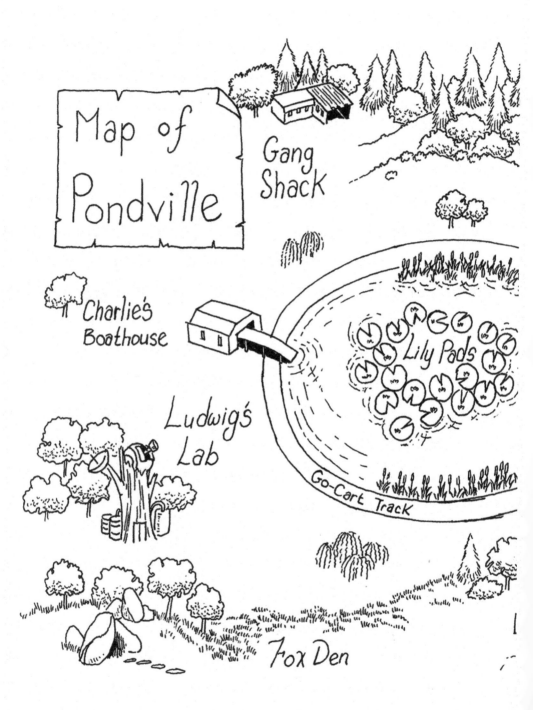

Harry's Cabin
N
E
S
W
Town Hall
Courthouse Jail
General Store
Hospital

# Chapter 1

The leaders of Pondville were in shock. Mayor Percy and Sheriff Harry had called a meeting of the region's mayors and deputy sheriffs. Pondville's Mayor Percy was the head mayor of the fifteen towns in the region and Harry served as their sheriff.

Everyone had gathered at the city hall and sat around the largest conference table.

Mayor Percy stood at the podium and banged his gavel. He was a tough turtle when the situation demanded it. "Quiet, please. Set aside your donuts and coffee cups. Let's get this meeting underway without distractions."

Many of them wiggled around trying to make themselves comfortable on the hard chairs.

Percy touched his heart and sighed. "We have serious problems in our delightful communities."

Most were not in the know and they wondered what the heck he was talking about.

"First, there was the robbery from Professor Ludwig's safe. Perpetrators stole most of the power source for Wreck."

A collective gasp arose from the attendees. A few were heard to ask questions, such as:

"What? I can't believe it!"

"What does it mean to our communities?"

"What does it mean to my town?"

"Who could have done such a dastardly deed?"

At that moment Wreck rolled in late for the meeting.

Mayor Percy greeted the sheriff's car. "Why, hello, Wreck. Nice of you to make it."

Wreck, headlights lowered, said, "I'm sorry for being late. I was out patrolling late last night, and some water leaked out of my engine. It caused a short circuit that stopped me cold. Thank goodness for Charlie. He brought along a hair dryer and dried everything off. He tightened up a few bolts, and after that I was as good as new."

Wreck had no sooner finished than Sheriff Harry the frog stood up.

"Mr. Mayor? I would like to mention at this time that I invited Jake and Clinger because of their success with Pondville's Good Citizen Chapter. If not for their mentoring and guidance, many youngsters in Pondville would have gone astray. As reformed robbers, these two raccoons have a lot to offer. Thank you, Mr. Mayor. Sorry for the interruption."

Mayor Percy nodded to Harry and Wreck. "Thanks for the information. Let's move on with the meeting. Wreck, if you have any questions about the first problem we covered, check with Harry."

Wreck said, "Will do, Mayor."

Percy checked his notes and continued. "Here's the second problem: a resident of Bridgetown is missing and is nowhere to be found. It hasn't happened in any other towns in our region … *yet*. Sooner or later, it could happen in Pondville or Lankasville or any of our other peaceful towns. I am

not trying to place fear into your hearts, but this is the reality we face. We need to sharpen our policing for the protection of our people and goods."

Mayor Sydney of Bridgetown piped up, "I couldn't agree more."

Others called out, "Hear, hear," and "Right on."

"Okay, settle down," commanded Percy as he banged his gavel on the podium. "I am now going to turn this meeting over to Sheriff Harry. Sheriff, it's all yours."

Harry got up, stood tall, and strode toward the podium. He shook hands with a few citizens on his way. He smiled and, in a strong hearty voice, said, "Good morning, everybody."

The audience returned a feeble "Good morning." Many were wide-eyed and mouthing "No, it is not."

It was obvious to Harry that most of them were stunned and bewildered.

"Listen up, everybody. Get your heads in the right place and keep your minds open." Sheriff Harry spoke with all the authority of his position. "I need your full and complete attention. Your opinions are important." *I need these folks to lighten up and pay attention.* "I don't mind if you continue drinking your coffee. It looks like you really need it. But please, no munching on the donuts. The munching throws off my thought process."

A few chuckles erupted.

"As Mayor Percy said, Bridgetown has a missing resident. Before this meeting, headquarters informed me that other towns just reported more missing residents." Harry leaned in and spoke almost in a whisper: "We suspect kidnappings. I briefly spoke to Arthur, the chief deputy sheriff of Lankasville. He and other deputy sheriffs are asking for additional help. We must find the missing residents and bring them home. Arthur, would you like to comment?"

The wolf stood slowly, visibly shaken. However, his strong arms and wide chest signaled that he would not be easily pushed around. "Sheriff Harry, thank you. We never thought this would happen in our peaceful town. Our residents are so afraid, they are keeping their young ones out of school. It's a bad situation and growing worse every day. Fear is paralyzing our community. We need help." Arthur sat down with a thud and let out a big huff.

"That certainly paints a vivid picture of what's happening. Thank you, Arthur," said Harry. "Right now we do not have enough deputies to protect Pondville, never mind the other towns in the region."

Harry looked each of the mayors in the eye and pointed at many of the deputies. "This is an issue for us to attack today. To put it mildly, I was stunned by the robbery at Professor Ludwig's lab."

A mayor asked, "How did the robbers break into the lab?"

"I don't know how that happened. I wish I did. However, we will get to the bottom of it. And now, all these missing residents … it's too much. By the way, most of them are youngsters."

Loud gasps and fearful cries erupted from the gathering.

Harry scanned the concerned faces and said, "This is what I propose: I want to form an investigative unit to focus on major crimes and kidnapping. It will be called the Pondville Bureau of Investigation, known as PBI."

Everyone spontaneously broke out in applause.

Harry raised a hand. "Hold on, folks. This may sound easy, but it requires the right team and intense organization to make it work. For example, this is why I invited Jake and Clinger to our meeting. As you well know, they were the perpetrators of the general store robbery. They have since reformed, and so have their cohorts. They helped in turning

Pondville into a more respectable place by their own example. They have mentored many of our youngsters to become model citizens. Given their outstanding leadership, they are the first two that I am appointing to our investigative staff."

Clinger the raccoon raised a hand.

"Yes, Clinger. Is there something you want to add?"

Clinger stood up to his full height and nodded to Harry. "Yes, Sheriff. On behalf of Jake and myself, we would be honored to serve. Thank you so much for your confidence and belief in us." He smiled as he sat down.

"You're welcome. You both deserve this new position. We still have openings for others interested in joining the PBI. Of course, all applicants will be thoroughly checked. I'll meet with Kim, Bart, and Arthur to figure out what we need to do to provide the best policing possible for all our towns. I will get back with you once I have a proposal. That's all I have for now, Mr. Mayor." Harry took his seat.

Percy walked back to the podium. "Thank you, Sheriff. Now I will entertain a few questions. I will limit them because we are going into uncharted areas."

Several hands shot up.

Percy said, "Yes, Mayor Sydney."

"What are the plans for these perps once they are captured?"

Percy responded, "I don't have a complete answer to that. It is something the Sheriff's Department will address. My assumption is the perps will be locked up in the Pondville jail. Next question."

"Are there any clues on the robbery or the kidnappings?" asked another mayor.

"Not yet," Percy said. "We need the PBI to go to work. That's all, folks. I don't mean to cut anybody off, but I don't have any answers, as you can tell. With that, I am closing the meeting. I'll let you know when our next meeting will be."

***

As they walked out, Kim, Bart, and Arthur huddled with Harry.

"Let's reassemble in my office in an hour," Harry said. "We need to put our heads together about the PBI so we can have it up and running immediately. Please invite Stinky, Earl, Jake, and Clinger to attend. I'll see you in an hour."

Chief Deputy Sheriff Kim said, "Roger that."

# Chapter 2

"Get my sunglasses," demanded Rolf. "That darn sun is too bright. It's hurting my eyes."

"Here you go, Boss," said Joey, flipping the sunglasses to Rolf, who caught them one-handed.

Sunlight shone through cracks in the walls of the Wolf Gang's shack. Joey, Thor, Blackie, and Brownie sat around the wooden table eating breakfast with Rolf. They were the core group of the gang, Rolf's go-to guys.

Pizza was their favorite food and they devoured it. They also chewed on bones, making loud crunching sounds. Bones gave added flavor to the cold pizza. As usual, their chewing was noisy and broken by a few burps here and there. And then there was the slurping of their sodas. Only bad manners in this clubhouse!

Rolf leaned back in his chair. He finished the last morsel of food and breathed a loud sigh of pleasure.

Rolf's breath was bad—so bad it could knock anyone over in a second—but it did not bother his four cohorts. In fact, their breath was just as bad. No one even bothered to duck when one of them breathed out. What a predicament for anyone other than the wolves sitting there.

"So, Boss," Blackie asked, "where are we heading and what are your plans in general?"

Rolf sneered and said, "I haven't forgotten what that Pondville community did to me, and they will pay ... oh, how they will pay." He huffed and puffed with his cheeks flapping wildly. His eyes bulged.

The gang could almost hear his heart pumping.

"What's the status of our new fortress, Thor? How's it coming along?" Rolf's beady eyes glowed as he questioned his head builder.

The wolves could hear the excitement in Rolf's voice.

"It should be finished in a week or so," responded Thor. He stuck his well-built chest out when he spoke. "We're now digging a moat around the fortress and we'll fill it with water. By the way, Rolf, the water will come from a large stream that fills the Pondville pond. We'll have to figure out how to divert it to our moat."

"I've got that covered," Rolf said in his rough, growling voice. "You are going to love my idea. I've highjacked a beaver colony to build a dam that will block the stream and divert it to the moat. Those toothy beavers know the consequences if they don't follow my orders. They won't dare go against me."

"Brilliant," said Thor.

With a big smirk, Rolf said, "Won't Pondville be surprised when the water in the pond starts to go down. Take that, you slimy frogs."

The rest of the gang laughed and howled. They were Rolf's cheering squad.

Basking in their admiration, he continued. "What about the lookout towers on the top of the fortress? Are they ready? Have you tried them out?"

"They're coming along slowly." Thor exhaled a big sigh. "We could use more help to speed up progress."

"That's easy," Rolf snapped back. "Kidnap more citizens, as many as we need."

"Even if we kidnap more, we don't have enough room to keep them. We're running out of space, especially in the dungeon. Here's the good news. So far, no one has escaped and been able to give away our secrets or our position. Fear has been successfully drummed into them. They know what will happen if they escape and are caught."

"Good. Fear is my favorite option," Rolf said, eyeing his gang. "If someone gets out of hand, make the fool go without food. I know there is a limit on the food thing, because we need to keep them strong and fairly healthy. You know what to do."

He turned his focus on his head builder. "Thor, stay on schedule as best you can."

"Boss, can I ask you another question? About the stupid rocks we stole from the lab."

"Sure, what's the question?"

"Why did we steal them and what're they for?"

"One thing's for sure, boys. If Ludwig kept the rocks locked up, they must be valuable. They seem to have the power to cause weird things to happen with anything around them."

"When I picked up the rocks," Blackie piped in, "their eerie colors really spooked me."

Rolf stroked the hairs on his chin and said, "I mean to find out everything about those rocks. I want to know where the power is coming from. Is it from the rocks? How come nothing happens when we touch the rocks? If the rocks have power, how is it activated? How can it help us? I will get answers.

Right now, I think Ludwig the turtle is the only one who has the secret."

"Agreed. Ludwig probably knows the most," said Thor. "After all, he is a genius and always coming up with something new."

Rolf sneered. He growled and said, "I know, I know. When I saw that stupid car flying and doing things I've never seen before, it blew my mind. I mean to find out why these weird things are happening with that car."

Joey chimed in. "Yeah, maybe it's the rocks. If it is the rocks, they can help us conquer Pondville. Then we could make it our community, all to ourselves."

Rolf loved this idea so much, he rubbed his paws together gleefully. "I'll make them pay for humiliating me and making me spend time in jail. Not only that, but those creeps also took away my chance to win the derby race. I was a shoe-in. Everyone who was connected with the go-cart derby will pay."

# Chapter 3

It was time to talk about the PBI. Crowded into Harry's office were: Kim the deer, a chief deputy sheriff of Pondville; Bart the bear, another chief deputy sheriff; Jake, the reformed raccoon; Clinger, another reformed raccoon; Arthur, the chief deputy sheriff of Lankasville; Stinky the skunk, a deputy sheriff of Pondville; and Earl the crow, another deputy sheriff. They eagerly awaited the discussion.

Harry said, "Thank you for getting together so quickly."

"I wouldn't miss this meeting for anything," said Earl, perched on a chair back. "You know, Harry, not only are crows smart, but we are super curious also."

"Good to know, Earl," said Harry, grinning at the deputy. "Our region has grown from seven towns to fifteen in the past couple of years. There is at least one deputy sheriff in each town, and, as you all know, Pondville is the hub of the region. We're stretched thin whenever there is a crisis."

Chief Deputy Arthur said, "Don't I know it, Harry."

"So, here's what I'm thinking," said Harry. "We usually can handle emergencies, small crimes, and those in progress. Remember how well we dealt with the robbery at the Pondville General Store?"

"I'll never forget it," said Clinger, with a smirk. "My time spent in jail was a real wake-up call."

Everybody laughed, including Clinger.

Kim said, "I'm amazed how you've turned your life around."

Bart said, "That was a doozy of a crime and we made a brilliant arrest."

"Enough trips down memory lane, you guys," said Harry. "We are facing our worst crime situation ever. No one has a clue about the identity of the perps or what's next. We have a major heist and several kidnappings to deal with. We need crack investigators and that is what the PBI is all about."

"When we are in the thick of trouble, how can we take time to form a new unit, Harry?" asked Stinky. This skunk had a sharp mind.

Harry smiled, thinking, *Stinky always asks great questions.* "Sometimes," he replied, "you have to just do it. I want to start it, at the very least. Now, why did I pull all of you together? Because you think clearly and don't always agree with me! I know I can count on you. Besides, most of you make us laugh and we need that when times are tough."

Harry paced around the room with his hands clasped behind his back. "I'll throw out ideas and you react. The PBI will be led by Kim and Arthur, to start. The mission will be to investigate major crimes and kidnappings that occur anywhere in our region. Jake and Clinger will be the first trainees, learning all the ins and outs of investigating. We will add others as we grow."

"But what will they do if there are no major crimes or kidnappings?" asked Bart.

"That's an easy one, Bart. They'll do policing, like the rest of the sheriff's deputies."

"Won't Arthur and I need a lot of time to set this up?" asked Kim. She had jotted lots of notes and quite a few questions in her police notebook.

"Yeah. How can I take the time to do this when I'm already investigating Lankasville's missing residents?" asked Arthur, with a scowl.

"Hold on, hold on. I know the timing is bad, but it is also good. Every deputy in the region will be working on the kidnappings and robbery, as well as their routine duties. We can learn new techniques while dealing with this crisis. This will almost be a training ground for the PBI."

Jake asked, "Will members of the PBI also continue regular duties?"

"Yes. That is exactly what you'll do. Think of our current situation as on-the-job training for the future."

Kim asked, "So what do you expect us to accomplish for the PBI during this time?"

"You tell me. What do you think you can do?"

Jake spoke up. "We could figure out which techniques work best when solving a crime … and the best way to do them. Then we can share that information with everyone and with new recruits."

"I like it," said Arthur. "We do our jobs, and while we're at it we find better ways for doing investigations."

"Honestly," said Harry, "that's probably all you can do while we deal with this crisis."

"We can do one more thing," Kim said. "We can identify outstanding recruits for the PBI. Certain deputies will shine at investigating and solving crimes."

"Good point, Kim. Now we know some things we can do to get the PBI going. Once the current situation is under control, we'll meet again. Sound like a plan?"

All agreed.

"Let's head out. Stay safe."

# Chapter 4

Ludwig the turtle popped into Harry's office, a little out of breath. "Did you want to see me?"

"Yes, Professor. I'd like to do some training exercises and dry runs with Wreck. We need to be sure he can do the things required for his job. I'll need your help."

Ludwig said, "No problem. Great idea. You don't want to wait until there is an emergency to find out whether or not he can perform exactly as needed."

"Appreciate your cooperation, Ludwig. Right now, Wreck is over in his garage taking an afternoon nap. It's time to wake him up. Let's go."

It took them a few minutes to reach the garage.

Harry opened the garage door and called out, "Yoo-hoo, Wreck, are you awake? We need to do some work."

No response ... only the sound of a soft hum resembling a snore.

Ludwig walked over to Wreck and tapped gently on a fender, so as not to startle him.

Wreck, sleepy-eyed, said, "Uhh, uhh ... what, what? What's going on? You spoiled the wonderful dream I was having. I was at a place beyond belief: on a beautiful beach with the waves lapping at the shore. I was relaxing, watching youngsters playing and riding the surf. It felt so wonderful."

Harry said, "I'm sorry, Wreck, but we have work to do."

Good-naturedly, Wreck said, "What's important enough to ruin my dream? It had better be good."

"This is serious. Put aside that nice dream," Harry said in his best sheriff's voice. "Ludwig and I want to go over some maneuvers that you'll have to do when the need arises. And the need could arise at any moment. You're aware of what's happening in our region, so let's get cracking."

Wreck shuddered. "Maneuvers. Oh great, just what I need. I'm really not in the mood. Besides, it sounds scary."

Ignoring Wreck's attitude, Harry said, "All right, all right, roll out so we can get in."

"I guess I have to," Wreck mumbled, and slowly turned his wheels.

Harry and Ludwig hopped into the car, Harry at the controls and Ludwig sitting shotgun.

Ludwig asked Wreck, "How are you doing?"

"Oh, fine. I'm a bit nervous right now, wondering what you guys have in store for me."

"Hey, not to worry. Don't forget, Ludwig and I are in here. If things go south, we also suffer the consequences."

Wreck said, "Yeah, that's true. I'm okay with that. Let's do it."

Harry stepped on the pedal and pushed the joystick forward, moving Wreck ahead. Everything was smooth so far. Harry pulled the joystick up, and Wreck rose straight up. Then Harry pushed it forward again. They were flying.

Wreck said, "So far, so good. I can deal with this."

Harry shifted the joystick sideways, and Wreck moved to the right.

They practiced all kinds of exercises with Wreck staying in an upright position.

"I like this. How cool can this be?"

Harry said, "Okay. This is just a start. The basics are out of the way. Let's get down to business, Wreck. We're going to do some diving maneuvers, so ready yourself."

"Oh no, that sounds dangerous. Give me a break."

"Come on, Wreck, man up. No time for that."

"Oh, please, please be careful, Harry," said Wreck. "You know I am a delicate soul. And I want to stay that way."

Ludwig didn't say a word. The turtle tried to act cool, hoping his stomach wouldn't do flip-flops when they started to dive.

Harry glanced at Ludwig and said, "Tighten your seat belt—in case."

Wreck said, "Oh boy, that didn't sound good. What about my seat belt?"

Harry said, "Make sure your parachute is ready."

Wreck screamed, "What! What!"

"I'm kidding, I'm kidding."

Harry pulled up the joystick, and Wreck rose to an altitude of 200 feet to prepare for a dive.

Harry put the controls in a dive position, and down they went.

"Oh no, oh no!" screamed Wreck.

On the way down, Harry felt a bump in the joystick.

Ludwig held on for dear life. *I hope I don't hurl, I hope I don't hurl. Please, please, don't let me hurl.*

After Harry leveled off, Wreck called out, "Wow, that was fun. Can we do it again?"

"Hang on," said Harry. "I need to set you down so Ludwig can make a slight adjustment. Besides, he looks really green."

Once down, Ludwig sighed, relieved to be on solid ground again. He hopped out and opened the hood. Being on the ground allowed his stomach to settle down. "Okay, Sheriff, what was it you felt?"

"It felt like a vibration coming up through the joystick."

"Good. Let me see. Ah, yes, there are a few bolts that have loosened." Ludwig took a wrench, tightened a few nuts and bolts, and adjusted a loose wire.

Wreck said, "Wow. What did you just do? It felt so good."

Ludwig looked up and said to Harry, "I think we are all set."

Wreck asked, "Was there anything wrong that I have to worry about?"

"No, everything's fine. I made an adjustment."

"That's good. It takes away my worry," said Wreck. "You know how I worry, after what I've been through."

Harry said, "All right, come on, guys, let's continue. We must get this right."

The rest of the afternoon they practiced all types of maneuvers, until Wreck did everything properly. Wreck was exhausted; still, he was okay with doing the training. The good news for all of them was that Ludwig did not hurl.

Sally the frog was sitting alongside the pond, watching their maneuvers, and wondering what the heck they were doing. "Are they playing?" she said to herself. "As they say, boys will be boys!"

After finishing the maneuvers, Wreck landed on the racetrack and moved over to where Sally was sitting.

Ludwig said, "Hey, Sally, nice to see you. You look very comfortable."

"Yes, I am. Good observation," she said with a wink. "You guys were doing some pretty daring stunts. What's up?"

Wreck said, "Yeah, did you see all my different maneuvers?"

"Yes, most of them. They were awesome."

Wreck said, "Weren't they cool?"

Sally smiled and nodded.

"Those maneuvers were a training session," Wreck said. "When we encounter bad guys who are trying to be cagey, we'll be ready for them."

Harry grinned and said, "You bet we'll be ready. We can never do enough practice to make sure we've got it right."

Ludwig chimed in, "This also proves that Wreck is up for the job. A fine specimen he is."

Wreck's chrome sparkled and he stated, with great humility, "Thank you, guys. I always try to do my best."

"All right, let's head back to my office. I need to write up some reports for today."

Harry waved, saying, "Later, Sally."

# Chapter 5

Ludwig had a new mission: find a way to transport someone from place to place using an aerial device. He worked nonstop in his lab. Right beside him was Tilly, his new apprentice. She was Bart's niece. Though still a bear cub, Tilly herself was showing signs of being a science genius.

"Tilly, help me to put this jetpack together."

"Certainly, Professor."

"This will revolutionize policing. It has built-in operating controls that will allow any deputy to fly on his or her own. Even your uncle Bart!"

"Really, Professor? I'm sure he's going to like that."

The jetpack was powered by X-rocks. There was only one problem. Ludwig was almost out of X-rocks due to the robbery; he did not have enough to finish his project.

"Tilly, would you please tie up any loose ends in the lab while I go looking for more X-rocks?"

"Certainly, Professor. I'd be happy to."

Never one to lose any time, Ludwig went up the hill to find more X-rocks. Hiding in the bushes were two spies from the Wolf-Pack Gang. Curiosity got the best of them.

Blackie turned to Joey and said, "Do you think he is up to something about those rocks? Let's follow him. Watch where you step. We don't want to alert him. All he needs to hear is a twig snap and he'll know someone is following him."

When Ludwig neared the X-rock area, he spotted Red, the general of the red ant army. He was leading his platoon on patrol.

Red was calling out a cadence: "Hup, one, two, three, four. Hup, one, two, three, four."

Ludwig smiled at their precision as they marched. Seeing Red and his platoon again gave Ludwig a warm feeling inside. Last year Ludwig had met Red for the first time. He knew how well the red ant army protected him in their territory.

At Ludwig's approach, Red's antennas alerted him that his territory was being breached. His built-in processor let him know it was Ludwig.

Red called out, "So, Sir Professor Ludwig, how are you doing today?"

"Just fine, General."

"What are you up to on this fine day? Anything my men and I can do for you?"

Ludwig replied, "Oh, I'm just up here to find some stinkweed for my project. I'm sure you remember that weed has an element which wipes out a deadly virus that kills turtles." Previously, Ludwig had used this story about stinkweed as his excuse to explore in the area, without giving up that he was really looking for X-rocks.

Red said, "Sure do."

Ludwig trusted the ants with his life. And he also knew that keeping X-rock secret was critical.

"Thank you for the offer, Red, but I'm okay for now. I don't need any help." He looked around and exclaimed, "Wow! I can't believe what you have done with this area. Your colony is really protected now, with all the outposts scattered about."

"Thank you for noticing. Yes, our living quarters are well guarded. So are the areas we promised you that we would protect," said Red. "None of us will ever forget how you saved our queen's life. By the way, how do you like being one of our knights?"

"Red," he responded with one claw over his heart, "it is one of the greatest honors of my life." Ludwig was a humble turtle; even so, being royalty was very special.

The queen was so grateful for Ludwig's rescue last year that she had immediately knighted him and put him under the colony's protection.

"Good to hear that, sir," replied Red.

"Thanks again for your support," said Ludwig as he tipped his beret. "I'll be on my way."

"Take care, sir."

Ludwig proceeded to his secret area and started scratching around for X-rocks.

Meanwhile, the spying wolves stayed far enough away so they wouldn't be seen. Inch by inch, they moved closer to see what Ludwig was doing. They figured something big must be up.

All of a sudden, horns and sirens blared. Red's army of fire ants had spotted the wolves, got into attack position, and charged. The fire ants surrounded the unwelcome intruders and climbed all over them, biting, scratching, and stinging them all over their bodies. The assault was relentless. Yelling and screaming, the wolves ran back toward their shack. The pain was unbearable and wouldn't stop. All they wanted to do was get away as fast as possible.

Ludwig heard the commotion, but didn't pay any attention to it. He felt safe and secure knowing Red had his back. He kept on digging and scraping, determined to find more X-rocks. In no time, he found an ample supply, quickly dug it up, and filled his backpack. Before leaving, he filled in the area where he had been digging so it wouldn't look as if it had been disturbed. *Time to head back.*

On the way to his lab, Ludwig bumped into Red. "Hey, General, what was that commotion all about?"

Red wore a stern look, put his hands on his hips, and said, "There was a breach of our perimeter. Boy, did they pay for trespassing!"

Ludwig asked, "Did you see who they were?"

"Sure. Two wolves. I'm sure they won't come back after that attack. Last I saw of them, they were running away, screaming and howling in pain. That'll teach them to respect private property."

Ludwig smirked, picturing the scared wolves. "Thank you again for your protection."

"Sir Ludwig, we did it for the protection of our home, as well as for your supply of stinkweed. Nobody fools with us."

Ludwig said, "I can certainly understand. I need to go now and finish up an important project. See you guys later."

On the way back to his lab, Ludwig wondered, *Who are they? Are they following me, and where are they from? Oh well, hopefully there is nothing to be concerned about.*

Little did he know they were members of Rolf's Wolf-Pack Gang.

Ludwig went inside his lab and locked the door before unpacking his treasure.

Tilly was busy finishing her assigned project. She looked up and said, "Oh, you're back. Did you find enough X-rocks to finish our project?"

"Sure did. Help me unload my backpack. I want to finish up the rest of the jetpacks."

They worked several hours fine-tuning his latest invention.

Finally, he was satisfied they had dealt with all the loose ends. Ludwig slapped his hands together twice, turned to Tilly, and said, "We have finished! Help me put the leftover rocks away."

They carefully placed the X-rocks into the safe, and Ludwig activated the new security system.

The professor rubbed his chin, thinking, *Now, to try my invention, all I need is a test pilot.*

# Chapter 6

Ludwig ran to the sheriff's office. Tilly trailed him, carrying a jetpack.

He was so excited, he couldn't wait to show Harry his newest invention. Peeking into Harry's office, he asked, "Am I interrupting anything? I see that Stinky, Jake, Hapless, and Earl are here."

Harry said, "No, that's okay. Come on in. I expect that Bart and Kim will be joining us any minute. We plan to go over some police procedures."

As if on cue, Bart and Kim strolled in.

"Hi, everybody," said Kim. "Looks like we have quite a crowd here."

Bart said, "I'll say. Even my niece."

"Hi, Uncle," said Tilly, grinning. She was eager to have him see how well she was doing as Ludwig's apprentice.

"Take a seat, everybody," said Harry. "Ludwig, what have you got for us?"

"You see, something really bothered me," Ludwig said to start off. He removed his glasses and continued. "What if a perp was making a fast getaway and you had trouble catching up with him, especially if he went into the woods and bushes. So I put on my thinking cap."

"Professor, I don't think you ever take that cap off," Sheriff Harry said with a chuckle. "Let's hear what you have for us this time."

"A jetpack."

*Whoa* ... everyone waited in anticipation to see what the local genius had just invented.

Ludwig said, "I came up with this jetpack system. It'll give your deputies a tremendous advantage. They will be able to fly on their own!"

"You're joking, right, Professor?" said Bart, hoping the opposite.

"No, I'm not. It has the same power system as Wreck's, but much more condensed. I happen to have one here."

With eyes wide open, everybody leaned in for a better look at the jetpack.

Harry looked at it closely and said, "This sounds amazing. It looks nice and compact. It would certainly give us a big advantage over any perp who might be flying into the trees or bushes to evade capture."

Most of them nodded.

"Hey, not me," said Earl the crow. "I can fly around without one of those."

Everyone laughed.

"How does it work?" asked Kim. "And how can it work the same for all of us? Look how different we are."

Ludwig explained. "As I said before, it works on the same principles I used to develop Wreck's new power system. With Tilly's help, let me demonstrate and show you the key parts. It's very simple. Tilly will strap it on her back to show how it's done."

Tilly quickly put the pack on and adjusted the straps to fit snugly. She nodded and smiled at the group.

"How does it feel on your back, Tilly?" asked Ludwig.

"I can easily handle the weight and size. With the straps adjusted, it feels comfortable."

Ludwig said, "It has a joystick on the right and the speed control lever on the left. You can activate the pack by pushing the button on top of the joystick. Any questions so far?"

Stinky said, "Yes. How heavy is the jetpack?"

"Surprisingly light," responded Ludwig. "The pack is custom made to adjust to the size of each deputy. For example, Bart would have a large pack, whereas Jake would have a smaller one."

In awe, Jake spoke up. "That's brilliant, Ludwig."

"What I would like to do is try the jetpack out today," said Ludwig. "Who would like to volunteer to test one out?"

"Why don't I try it," volunteered Harry. "After all, I'm familiar with Wreck's setup. I wouldn't need much instruction."

"Good thinking, Sheriff," said Ludwig.

"Okay, everybody, let's go outside." Harry was beaming.

"Here, Harry, this jetpack is just right for you. Tilly will help you put it on."

Tilly helped Harry while Ludwig watched carefully to make sure they did it right.

"How does it feel on you?" asked Ludwig.

"Comfortable."

"Good. Let's make sure the straps are snug because they hold the controls. You need to be certain you can access them easily." Ludwig tugged on the straps to see if they were secure. Next he checked to make sure Harry could reach the controls. "There. You are good to go. Take it away, Harry."

The sheriff pushed the red button to turn it on. He placed his hands firmly around the speed lever and the joystick. He pulled up on the joystick and pushed down on the speed lever. He shot up twenty-five to thirty feet in a few seconds, which made him gasp. He immediately put the joystick in neutral and hovered above everyone.

He called down, "I'm okay. That really took my breath away."

They clapped and cheered. Now they were eager to try it for themselves.

Ludwig said, "Before you descend, try moving sideways."

"I'll try and see what happens. The controls are very sensitive. I need to get used to them."

"That's the way I designed it, in case you have to make a fast getaway," said Ludwig.

"Here I go …." Harry moved at the same speed as he went up. He stopped and hovered again. "Instead of a lead foot, I think I have a lead hand."

Many of them laughed, Kim the loudest. She knew firsthand what a fast driver Harry was. And, after all, he had the nickname of Hurry-Up Harry.

Ludwig said, "Come on down, Harry. I need to adjust the speed lever."

"Why?"

Ludwig said, "I want to make it manageable for everyone."

"I'll come down, but I like it up here. This jetpack can really move. This is fantastic, unbelievable," Harry said, with the biggest grin. *I love the freedom,* he thought.

On the ground, Harry watched closely as Ludwig made adjustments. "Don't adjust it too much, Ludwig. I like it the way it is." *I may want to make some adjustments of my own!*

# Chapter 7

Joey and Brownie had watched, open-mouthed, as Harry jetted around. The wolves had hidden on the hill. Joey was still smarting from the red ant bites. Like a real trooper, he toughed it out.

"I can't believe what I'm seeing," Joey had whispered. "This is unbelievable. I've got to get back and let Rolf know what's going on. Brownie, you stay here and watch in case there is more happening we need to know about." Joey ran back to the shack to tell Rolf.

As he approached the gang shack, Joey saw Rolf sitting in the front yard with the wolf pack, and yelled out, "Boss, Boss, I have troubling news. You won't believe what we saw."

Rolf stood, crossed his arms, and snarled. "What have you got? Spit it out."

Joey paused for a second to catch his breath. "The sheriff was flying around, using something on his back. It was unreal. Never in a million years have I seen anything like this!"

Rolf put up one of his big paws, almost touching Joey's face. "Whoa, whoa. It seems to me as if those Pondville slimeballs are becoming more powerful with all their new gadgets. Who knows what's next?"

"Maybe it has something to do with Ludwig's stupid rocks," said Blackie.

"Hmm … that's really a good point."

Blackie added, "We stole all the rocks we could find in his lab. I bet he found more the other day when he went walking up on the hill. Joey and I were following him, but we could not move in close enough to see what he was doing. Fire ants attacked us." Blackie stooped to scratch his leg. "We had to retreat to save our lives."

Rolf rubbed his hairy chin and said, "I'm starting to put all of this together. One and one make two. Somehow, Ludwig suckered the ants into protecting the source of those rocks. Those fire ants will prevent us from getting our own supply. There is no doubt in my mind that we have to kidnap Ludwig. We have to convince him to give us the answers to the secret of the rocks. These mysterious gadgets … I've got to admit he is a genius."

They all nodded in agreement.

Just then, Brownie returned to the shack. "I left my lookout post as soon as everyone went into the sheriff's office. They were all patting Ludwig on the back and saying 'Nice work' and thanking him. My guess is they went inside for a secret meeting. No need for me to hang around."

Rolf paced around the shack. He stopped abruptly and said, "We've got to move up our plans. Thor, is that fortress done yet?"

"Almost done, Boss. We can move in there now if you want. The beavers finished building the dam. The water at the pond must really be dropping a bunch by now."

Rolf said to his crew, "Good. Let's pack up and move to our new headquarters."

The wolves moved sneakily through the woods. When they approached the fortress, Rolf and the others stopped and looked. Their eyes lit up when they saw their new home.

Rolf threw his arms wide and yelled, "Doesn't it look great? I love the towers on each corner. They're excellent lookout spots. I can observe the area all around the fortress. We'll be able to spot anybody trying to sneak in."

With pride, Joey said, "Take a look at the moat."

Rolf moved in for a closer inspection, and shouted, "And the moat ... wow! Nobody will get into our fortress. With the drawbridge up, anybody who tries to swim across will meet spikes sticking out from the bottom and a few more surprises. Brilliant! Come on, let's go inside. I want to see the finished product."

Thor clicked his remote control to lower the drawbridge, and the wolves trotted over it. Then they passed through a gate in the stone wall and entered a courtyard. It was an open area large enough for a small army to do practice drills. So far, everything was exactly what Rolf had envisioned.

From the courtyard, there were high wooden doors that opened inward to the main part of the fortress. They creaked when Joey and Brownie pushed them open. The first thing the wolves saw was a long hallway with corridors jutting out from it. Some led downstairs and some to other rooms. At the end of the hallway was the throne room. This was Rolf's masterpiece. Here he would greet guests, captives, or anyone who wanted an audience with him. Rolf surveyed the throne room. He pictured entertaining anybody brought to him—friend or foe. The throne was on a platform trimmed with gold and bright colors.

Rolf stood there with his chest out, beaming from ear to ear. "Gentlemen, we have arrived. From here, we will go out and conquer Pondville and other towns. Before you know it, the whole region will be under our control. We must get organized. Let's head to the conference room and strategize."

When inside, they each took a seat, with Rolf at the head of the table. The conference table was made up of four wooden barrels with long planks across for a tabletop. They made themselves at home, slouching in their chairs, some with their feet on the table.

Rolf said, "Okay, guys, this is what I want you to do. We need more gang members. We have to become larger and stronger to defend our new home and ourselves."

"Good idea, Boss," said Blackie. "We don't have the same weapons as those jerks on the so-called police force. But that will change as soon as we capture their weapons and make them our slaves."

"That's right," said Rolf, pounding a fist on the table. "We must outnumber them. Then we can overpower them with sheer numbers. Here is my plan. You'll infiltrate the surrounding communities and kidnap some wolf pups. We'll train them to become part of our force."

"But, Rolf, won't they spot us and bring in the police?"

"Yes, if you go in as one large group. I want you to split up into small units, go into their communities, gain their trust, and then capture the young ones. The younger, the better."

# Chapter 8

Three jetpacks were ready. Ludwig rounded up Charlie the frog, famous for his building skills, and Tilly, to help him make more. They worked quickly and quietly in his lab.

When the necessary quantity of jetpacks were made, sorted, sized, and labeled, Ludwig asked Charlie to let Harry know the jetpacks were ready. The professor had one more surprise in store for Harry and his deputies.

Charlie went to the sheriff's office and alerted Harry. "We're ready to go."

"Great," said Harry. "I'll gather the deputies and we'll head to Ludwig's."

***

All the deputies were assembled at the lab. Charlie and Ludwig outfitted them, with Tilly making a few adjustments here and there.

Bart said, "How do I look, Stinky?"

"Like a super-duper police professional." Stinky gave him a thumbs-up.

Harry helped Jake secure his jetpack. "How does that feel, Jake? Can you reach the controls easily?"

"Sure can, Sheriff."

Everyone had their jetpacks on and soon they would go outside for training. This was the first time they would fly on their own, except for Harry, of course.

Harry said, "Let's have a round of applause for Ludwig, Tilly, and Charlie."

They clapped and a few whistled.

Now was another big moment for the fearless inventor. Ludwig reached into his backpack and pulled out a square packet with a handle.

Harry said, "What in the world do you have there, Ludwig? Another invention?"

"Well, I got to thinking. What happens when your deputies encounter a bunch of perps that could overcome our security forces? Pondville could be in some real deep trouble."

Bart smiled at the brilliant turtle and said, "Ludwig, do you ever stop thinking? When do you rest?"

Ludwig answered in a serious tone. "Hardly ever. Anyway, I got to thinking. What if I devised a handheld unit that shot out a powerful ray which subdued a perp instantly?"

Stinky said, "You've got to be kidding, Professor. It can do that?"

"I'm not kidding. A perp wouldn't be able to resist or fight back. The force would render the perp momentarily powerless. Then they could be handcuffed, brought back to jail, and locked up. Meet the Stun-erator. Let me demonstrate."

He raised the device slowly. Everybody ducked and hit the floor out of fear that it might accidentally go off.

Ludwig had to chuckle. "Relax, everyone. The unit has to be activated in order to operate."

Sighs of relief filled the room. Everybody settled down.

"I need a volunteer to demonstrate the Stun-erator. Harry, how about you?"

"Oh no, not me, no way," said Harry. "It sounds too painful."

The other deputies murmured their agreement with Harry.

Bart said, "Flying is awesome. Getting stunned isn't."

"Hold on, you guys," said Ludwig. "Don't jump to conclusions. I wouldn't bring something here that would hurt you. Let's step outside so I can give you a demonstration."

As they gathered on the lawn, Harry knew he had to step forward. *After all, that's what a good leader would do.* "All right, Ludwig, I'll do it. You haven't put us in danger yet. But then again, I hope I don't have to take that back. Go ahead and try it out on me." Harry pulled his body straight, arms at his side. "I'm ready."

In his head, he believed Ludwig. In his heart, a screaming voice was saying, *Are you crazy!* Harry held his breath, waiting for Ludwig to shoot.

"Wait a second," Ludwig said. "Let me explain a little more."

Harry sighed in relief for the few more minutes before facing the decisive moment. His imagination went wild and his stomach churned, just thinking about what might happen.

"When the power source hits perps, it paralyzes them. They fall, not able to move."

Harry pushed his hat back, thinking, *Oh, great.*

"They're not hurt," said Ludwig. "In several minutes, they completely recuperate. By then they have been handcuffed and secured."

Kim said, "It sounds too good to be true, Ludwig."

"It isn't. Not to worry, Kim. Here, let me demonstrate how it works and how safe it is. This little switch activates the unit. Aim the unit at the perp, press the red button, and watch your perp go down." Ludwig aimed it at a nearby tree and pressed the red button. Nothing happened to the tree, proving that the force was not dangerous.

There was a lot of grumbling among the deputies:

"Yeah, right."

"Sure."

"Doubt it."

"No way, not me."

"I'm brave, but not that brave."

Ludwig asked, "Is there anyone else, besides the sheriff, who would like to volunteer?"

Everyone lowered their head and refused to make eye contact with Ludwig. So much for enthusiasm!

Bart moved forward and said, "Wait a minute. Hold on. Why don't I go first? I'm the biggest one here. If it works on me, it'll work on anybody. Harry, take that one off your plate right now. You're always the first one to volunteer. Let me take this one."

Harry smiled, more than a little relieved. He was proud of his chief deputy. "Great. Thank you for volunteering. All right now, stand over there in that nice soft grass. ... Are you ready?"

Bart nodded.

Ludwig turned the unit on, aimed it at Bart, and pressed the red button. They could see a spark-filled ball shoot out. Down he went, with a slight quiver, into a frozen position. The soft grass really broke his fall. Everyone ran to the brave bear.

Stinky asked his best friend, "Are you okay, Bart?"

Bart started to move and said, "Wow, yeah, I'm okay." He slowly got up with the help of Jake and Kim. He brushed himself off, astonished at what had happened.

Harry said, "That's amazing. This certainly proves it's reliable. We'll all feel confident now when we engage a perp who is strong and large. How long will it take for you to make us some of these units?"

"I'll have ten units ready in three days. Tilly is already working on it."

Jake exclaimed, "Imagine. We're able to fly with our own jetpacks, and with the Stun-erator we can take anybody down who commits a crime! Fantastic!"

***

Two of Rolf's henchmen had watched everything from their hiding spot.

Thor said, "What is it with this professor? Every time we turn around, he comes up with something new. He's unbelievable. Now they have something that shoots out a ray and paralyzes you! We've got to get back to Rolf and tell him about it. This is a game changer."

# Chapter 9

Rolf slurped his special herbal concoction. The drink made him feel powerful. He half reclined on his throne, his legs crossed over an arm. Two squirrels and an opossum, captured from Lankasville, were fanning him with large feathers.

Every couple of minutes Rolf would yell, "Faster." When he was satisfied, he would command, "Slower."

The captives were very young and had such sad looks on their faces. One squirrel whimpered softly, "I want my mommy."

The opossum scowled as he whispered, "When I am bigger and stronger, I'm going to wring Rolf's ugly neck."

"Did I hear you say something?"

"Oh no, sir. You may have heard me clearing my throat."

"That better be the case. You don't want to face the type of punishment I have in mind, do you?"

"Oh no, sir."

"All right. Carry on." Rolf settled back on his throne and finished his drink.

After relaxing for a while, Rolf straightened himself up. "Hey, anybody out there?"

Blackie ran into the room. "What's up, Rolf? Do you need anything?"

"Yeah, more wolf pups. Have they returned with any new recruits yet?"

"Boss, I just lowered the drawbridge for our men to enter and they had four in tow," said Blackie.

The gang members approached the throne, pushing the four terrified young pups along.

Rolf motioned to the squirrels and opossum fanning him, and said to Blackie, "Get these three out of here. I need private time to go over things with our new captives."

"Right away, Boss." Pointing to the three, Blackie said loudly, "Grab your fans and get out, *now*. Move. ... Move faster."

They scampered out as quickly as their short legs would take them.

The captured wolf pups clung together for comfort. They had fearful looks. They were shaking. One had tear tracks running down his face.

As soon as the others left, Joey stepped forward and said, "We kidnapped these four from Bridgetown. With training, I think they'll serve your purposes."

Rolf circled them and bellowed, "Attention, my young wolves. There is nothing for you to be afraid of. Get used to it, you are here to stay. Forget your mothers and fathers. They will never see you again."

Tears filled their eyes with the thought of never seeing their families again.

Rolf continued to bellow, "I own you. Do as we tell you. With the proper training, you can become one of us. We are your family now. Once your training is complete, the fun will begin. Okay, men, take them away and start training exercises pronto."

He made a shooing motion and said, "Blackie, any others back yet?"

"Some arrived with more captives."

"Good, we need more servants to do cooking and cleaning, and more wolf pups to train. That'll free us up to defend ourselves and carry out my plan to take over Pondville. Their peaceful life will be over, forever gone once we conquer them."

Blackie and Brownie flashed huge smiles, imagining the power they would have in Pondville.

"Blackie, go to the tower and fill my hot tub. I want to sit and soak while I plan our next move. And don't forget the bubble bath. I like to pop the bubbles one at a time. It clears my mind."

Rolf was dizzy from his drink. A bath would be a good way to clear his head.

Accompanied by Brownie, Rolf strolled to his private quarters. As he stepped up and into the tub, down he went in a belly flop. Water splashed everywhere. Brownie ran over to assist Rolf.

Blackie heard the commotion and rushed in to help. Together they pulled up their boss and settled him onto the seat.

Rolf snarled, "Back off. I'm okay."

Blackie and Brownie raised their arms and said, "Okay, Boss, okay. We just wanted to make sure you're all right."

"I'm fine, I'm fine. Fetch me some raw meat. And while you're at it, I'll have some toothpicks to clean my teeth."

# Chapter 10

Sheriff Harry had assembled ten deputies from the region. It was time to do practice drills with the new equipment. Bart and Kim would oversee the maneuvers to make sure they were done correctly. Harry and Wreck planned to watch from the sidelines of the Sheriff's Department back lot.

"Deputies," Kim said, "put on your equipment, and I will time you. Bart will go around to make sure it is on correctly. Got it?"

They nodded.

"All right now, on the count of three, put on your equipment. One, two, three." Kim started her timer.

Bart moved around, coaching them as needed. He couldn't help but grin when he saw the gyrations some of them were going through, trying to put their jetpacks on.

After the packs were on, Kim announced the best and worst times for their first go-round. "Speed is important, especially in an emergency, but putting it on correctly is also critical."

"Ditto," said Bart.

"Now," she said, "we are going to go through several rounds of the exercises to improve your timing. As before, Bart will circulate and help you as needed."

It took nine rounds to achieve satisfactory results. At last, they did it!

Kim smiled at the deputies and said, "Kudos. You are now ready to go at any time."

"Good job, deputies. You are dismissed," Bart said with a big toothy smile.

*** 

"They really did well with their exercises."

"I agree with you, Wreck. It won't be long before everybody is fully prepared. We'll get the remaining deputies in for the same kind of practice session. With that, we should be able to handle any serious situation."

Harry picked up his megaphone and called out, "Bart, Kim, could you come here for a minute?"

They jogged over, and Kim said, "What's up, Sheriff?"

"How do you think the practice drills went?"

"Really well," said Bart. "We'll have a session for the remaining deputies tomorrow. All will be up to snuff in no time."

Kim added, "I'm really proud of how well everybody is doing. They understand how important it is. I think you will find them practicing whenever they have a free moment."

"Yeah," said Bart. "I think there's competition to see who is the fastest."

Harry smiled and nodded.

*** 

Back at the boathouse, Charlie was talking to himself, as usual. "Looks great. I love the new tattoo on my boat. I've got to put the boat in the water to see how it looks from there. On second thought, I'd better wait. You know, the water level seems lower every day. Something's wrong! Enough. I've got to find Harry. We need to find the underlying cause of this. They had practice exercises this morning at the sheriff's back lot. I'll stroll over to see if Harry is still there."

\*\*\*

Charlie ambled over to the practice area. "Harry, glad I caught up with you. Hey, Wreck, Kim, Bart. Hope the practice was a success."

"It was," said Bart.

Kim smiled at Charlie while she was thinking, *He's always fun to have around.*

Charlie was not smiling. Clearly, he was on a mission. "Harry, have you noticed that the water level in the pond is still going down?"

"You know, Charlie, I have," answered Harry. "I thought it was because we haven't had much rain lately, but this is becoming ridiculous. If this continues and the pond dries up, it'll be a disaster for Pondville."

He turned to Bart and Kim. "Have either of you noticed anything unusual about the pond? Anything that might cause the pond to dry up?"

Bart said, "It seems strange that the water level is going down. I know we haven't had much rain. Usually, that's not a problem. The two streams, especially the big one, that feed the pond make up for a dry spell."

Before they finished talking about the pond, Chief Deputy Arthur arrived. "Sorry to interrupt, Sheriff. Have you got a second?"

"Sure, what's up?" asked Harry.

"We're reaching a crisis point in Lankasville. Young wolves are being kidnapped."

Bart asked, "How many are missing?"

"Four, at last count. They are very young … less than four months old."

Kim shook her head. *How awful.*

"Not only that," said Arthur, "but other towns are saying that their youngsters have disappeared. We are at our wits' end as to what to do."

Harry asked, "Have you sent out patrols?"

"Yes. Our patrols haven't encountered anything suspicious. Whatever they're doing is not obvious. Whoever is behind this is well organized. Strange thing about it ... they seem to know our every move. Then they strike when we are most vulnerable."

"Bridgetown also reported missing youngsters," Kim said.

"This has gone far enough," said Sheriff Harry as he stood with his arms crossed and his feet planted far apart.

"Bart, alert all deputies to meet at headquarters in one hour."

# Chapter 11

"Welcome, Deputies," said Harry. "We're here to bring everyone up-to-date on the latest happenings, especially in Lankasville and Bridgetown. I'll ask the deputy sheriff from Bridgetown to start off."

The deputy sheriff stood up and said, "The good news is that there are no new reports of children missing from our community."

"That is encouraging," Harry replied.

The deputy continued his report. "However, the residents are outraged and demanding results. They want their youngsters back. Our deputies are patrolling around the clock. Everything seems to be at a standstill. By the way, we are using the new equipment to stay up to speed. The jetpack gives us a good aerial view. If anything, this added vigilance has stymied criminal activity. So, most of the townsfolk feel safe at the moment."

Harry looked around at the other deputies. "Did you get that, everyone?"

They nodded.

"Sheriff, I don't know what more we can do to bring our missing kids back. I am at my wit's end." The deputy sheriff shrugged his shoulders and shook his head as he sat down.

Harry said, "Thank you, Deputy. Now let's hear from Lankasville."

Chief Deputy Arthur said, "Nothing unusual at this point. Everything is status quo. And I'm having the same issues as they are in Bridgetown. Residents are demanding results *now*. They want to know what we are doing to stop the kidnappings and bring our young ones back home safely."

Kim stood up, straightened her vest, and said, "If we don't get some results soon, residents are going to revolt, or worse, try to handle it themselves— vigilante style."

Harry said, "We certainly don't need that. I agree with Kim. Fear sometimes makes folks do crazy things."

"Jake, have you got anything unusual to report from Pondville?"

"No, Sheriff. It seems that the perps are laying low or have moved on. But where are they keeping the missing children? We have scoured the hills and woods and have found nothing. We even went to the wolf gang shack and nobody was there. It felt eerily quiet. Maybe they have moved on. Let's hope so."

Harry said, "We must stay vigilant and not let our guard down. Unfortunately, it's a waiting game. In time, somebody is going to mess up. That's when we'll strike. Anything can happen at a moment's notice. Is there anything else anyone would like to bring up?"

Charlie stood up. "Yes, Sheriff. I am sure all of you have noticed that the water level in the pond keeps dropping down slowly. We did have some rain in the past few weeks, but it didn't make any difference. It doesn't feel right. Something is going on that we don't know about. Just saying …."

"Well, Wreck and I conducted a search of the streams, and the large one has dried up almost completely," said Harry. "I don't have any answer for that. We'll broaden the search to see if anything is going on that we are not aware of. We need results. I don't know what else to say that hasn't been said already. Anything else?" He scanned the anxious faces. "No? Okay, keep up the good work, and keep your eyes and ears open. Dismissed."

*** 

Rolf and his crew sat around the conference table discussing their current situation.

"Joey, are you whipping those young pups into shape?"

"We sure are, Boss. You wouldn't recognize the difference in them from one day to the next. They are like sponges, absorbing everything. I expect them to be fully trained in the next few days."

"Super," said Rolf. "How efficient are they with bows and arrows?"

Joey confidently answered, "They can hit a target fifty yards away. They are ready. I'm really proud of them. Those pups are part of us now."

"I like everything you're telling me about them."

Joey continued. "Their past is their past and we are their future. There's no more bellyaching about going back home. They accept that their home is here. Their devotion and dedication are completely ours."

"Wonderful, Joey. You and your men have done an outstanding job with their training. We are ready to take the next step."

"What's that, Boss?"

At that moment Rolf's eyes bulged. The veins in his neck pulsated and the hairs on his neck stood up. He pounded so hard on the table that it shook.

With a fiery tone in his voice, he screamed, "I must get the skinny on how those stupid rocks work. We need to know what they can do for us. There is only one way to find out. That dopey professor figured out how to use them. So we need to capture him, bring him here, and wring it out of him. Instead of working for Pondville, we'll make Ludwig work for us."

"That's not going to be easy," said Blackie.

"Stay positive. That's an order."

Blackie lowered his head. "Yes, sir."

"Now, here's my plan," said Rolf. "I need two volunteers to come with me to capture Ludwig and bring him back. Who wants to accompany me to nab that so-called professor?"

Blackie's and Joey's arms shot right up, waving excitedly. Both wolves yelled, "Pick me, pick me." They wouldn't miss this for the world.

"Okay, Blackie and Joey, you're with me," said Rolf.

They high-fived each other.

Then Rolf laid down the law. "I want our stronghold on high alert. Brownie and Thor, make sure everybody else is in place and positioned to protect our fortress. Once we capture Ludwig, there will be an all-out force to find and free him. Sheriff Harry and his deputies will use everything in their arsenal to attack us. They will be relentless. We have to be prepared."

"Boss, don't forget their new equipment. I still can't believe they can fly around. Not only that! They also have a gadget that knocks you down and freezes you. What's next?"

"That's right. They have weapons and gadgets that are superior to ours. But we are smarter and more cunning than they are. We will take them down. Their weapons will be ours, but most of all, Pondville will be ours. Now, comrades, let us prepare for battle. You have your instructions. Let's move." Rolf waved to them to follow.

***

Within an hour Rolf and his henchmen crouched in the bushes, spying on Ludwig's lab. They were waiting for the right moment to kidnap him. Through an open window they observed the professor sitting at his lab table, having tea with Sally.

"Sally, what do you think about setting up a food bank for Pondville?"

"Great idea," said Sally, as she daintily picked up her teacup, pinkie extended.

Concerned, Ludwig said, "With the pond level dropping, our residents are having trouble growing food."

"You've got me thinking, Ludwig. We could contact Bridgetown, Lankasville, and other towns in the region and ask if they have any surplus items."

"Good idea, Sally."

"Why don't I start it up by asking a few residents to come with me to visit the other communities? Let's see what we can come up with." Sally was already in high gear.

Ludwig jumped up, knocking over his teacup. He put his index finger over his mouth as a signal to Sally. He whispered, "Wait a minute, did you hear something?"

"No, I didn't hear anything. What did you hear?"

"It sounds like somebody is outside, moving around. I hear twigs snapping and break—"

The door burst open. Rolf, Blackie, and Joey grabbed Ludwig and Sally and quickly tied their hands behind their backs.

Sally screamed at the top of her lungs, "Help, help, we are being kidnapped!"

Rolf put a gag in her mouth to stop her from screaming. Then they gagged Ludwig.

In his smarmiest manner, Rolf said, "What a pleasant surprise. We have two prize packages from Pondville in our clutches. Let's get out of here fast. No one is the wiser yet."

\*\*\*

The three wily wolves loped back to the fortress with their prisoners in tow. Blackie and Joey brought them to the dungeon. The victims' gags were removed, and they were chained and shackled.

"Ow, that's too tight," cried Sally. "You're hurting me, you bully."

"Oh, am I hurting your dainty little wrists? Too bad. Suck it up, lady." Joey bared his long teeth at her.

\*\*\*

Rolf sat on his throne, relaxing after the successful mission, and sipping a cool drink. He felt like the king of the hill. "Joey, bring me the prisoners."

Sally and Ludwig were marched up from the dungeon. They were handcuffed and chained.

As they entered the throne room, Rolf continued to act smarmy and said, "So nice to see you, but unfortunately not under the circumstances you would like."

Sally raised handcuffed hands and wagged her finger at Rolf. "You're not going to get away with this, you mangy old wolf."

"I would watch your mouth if I were you."

Sally stamped her foot as best she could despite the chains binding her ankles. "I will not watch my mouth. I'll say whatever I please."

"Gag her right now. I won't tolerate that kind of sass from somebody like her. She'll learn her lesson."

Blackie pushed the yucky gag back into Sally's mouth. She tried to speak; it came out garbled. Rolf had a good laugh.

"Professor Ludwig, welcome to my fortress. At least you're smart enough to keep your trap shut."

Rolf was acting as if he was a genial host, rather than the nasty brute he actually was.

"Don't count on it."

Rolf forged ahead. "You have mystery rocks. They do wonderful things that would be very helpful to me. I need to know the secret of those mystery rocks. By now I'm sure you realize I am the one who stole them."

"So you're the one, you sneaky old thief. A pox on you! You'll never wrestle that information out of me. No one knows the secret but me. I will never, ever, divulge it to you or anybody else."

"Oh, you think so, huh? Maybe not today, maybe not tomorrow, and maybe not this week. When I finish with you, you will beg me for forgiveness and you'll spill the beans."

Rolf waved his hands in dismissal. "Guards, take them away to the deep dungeons. No food or water for them. Let them stew for a while. By the way, gag that uncooperative professor. I don't want them talking to each other for the time being."

After the guards prodded the prisoners away, Rolf had a quick meeting with his most trusted followers.

"Listen up, guys. I am going to put together a ransom note to Harry, indicating my terms for Sally's release. No matter what, Ludwig will remain a prisoner in the dungeon until he gives us the info we need."

Rolf turned to the wolf who often served as his secretary. "Thor, write this down on my best paper. 'Dear Losers, .......' Once it's ready, I'll sign it. Then I want you to make sure Harry finds it. And don't get caught."

# Chapter 12

Charlie was on his dock, perched on a post, soaking up some rays. He thought, *Why don't I go see my friend Ludwig and catch up on the latest?*

***

Charlie approached Ludwig's lab. As he got closer, he noticed the door was slightly ajar. *That's odd.* He called out before walking in, "Professor Ludwig, are you here?" The frog gingerly took a step inside. Everyone in Pondville knew that Ludwig loved his privacy and never liked to be surprised.

Charlie called out again, "Professor, are you in here?" and still, no response. He kept walking around. *This is strange. It doesn't feel right. Tilly's not here either. Maybe she has the day off.* Finding no one, he left, shutting the door behind him. He hurried to the pond to see if he could find Ludwig. Not there. So he stopped by Sally's lily pad … no Sally. *This is weird. Something's not right.*

***

Now really worried, Charlie headed to the Sheriff's Department. He figured maybe Harry would know where they were. When Charlie walked in, Harry was at his desk, doing paperwork.

Harry looked up and smiled. "Hey, what's up, cuz? I'm glad you're here … I need an excuse to take a break."

Charlie said, in a shaky voice, "Have you seen Professor Ludwig today?"

"No, not since yesterday. Why do you ask?" Harry looked perplexed.

"I just went to his lab, and he is nowhere to be found. The door was open. We know the professor is not that careless. Looks as if Ludwig was having tea with someone. One of the cups was tipped over and the tea was spilled all over his papers. I'm really concerned." Charlie was pacing around as he spoke. "Oh, by the way, have you seen Sally?"

"Can't say that I have. She is usually on her lily pad at this time of the day."

"I already checked, and she wasn't there. You know Sally. She always makes her presence known around here, one way or another," Charlie said with a smirk.

"That's odd," said Harry, taking his hat off and sweeping back what little hair he had. "Now I'm concerned. Let's get Wreck and look around. It'll be quicker that way."

\*\*\*

In the meantime, Thor snuck down to Ludwig's lab and attached a ransom note to the door. He quickly crept away.

***

Wreck was soaking up sun outside of Harry's office.

Harry called out, "Wreck, have you got a minute?"

"Sure, what's up?"

"Sally and Ludwig seem to be missing. They're probably out doing their own thing. But I'm concerned because of what's been happening lately. Let's go out right now and look for them. I'll feel better once we find them."

Wreck said, "Oh my. Sure. Hop in, guys."

They rode around the pond, calling out Sally's and Ludwig's names.

No answer. They stopped by Sally's lily pad … no Sally.

Now Harry was worried. "Let's head to Ludwig's lab. Maybe they're there."

When Wreck pulled up to the lab, Harry noticed a note stuck to the door. "Charlie, grab the note while I go in and look around."

"Will do," said Charlie. He had goose bumps.

Harry shouted, "Professor Ludwig, are you here?"

"Harry, come outside," Charlie said in a distraught voice. "You're not going to believe what this note says."

Charlie read the note to Harry and Wreck.

Dear Losers,

We have kidnapped Ludwig and Sally. If you fools don't know any better, my advice to you lower-than-life losers is to do exactly what you are told, or there will be dire consequences. I will be in touch.

Sincerely yours,
Rolf the Great

In a shaky voice, Wreck said, "Oh no! We've got to do something—and fast."

Charlie croaked, "I'm with you, Wreck."

"Hold on, you guys," Harry said. "Let's not panic. Settle down. The good news is we now know what we're dealing with. Those wolves are probably the ones responsible for all the kidnappings. The bad news is we must capture them without doing harm to their captives. Let's go to headquarters and sound the alert for all deputies to report immediately. We'll let the mayors know that they should attend also."

# Chapter 13

The deputies and mayors arrived in a hurry. Harry greeted them quickly and began to fill them in on the latest. "Attention! We have a crisis on our hands. Rolf and his gang kidnapped Professor Ludwig and Sally. Rolf left a ransom note saying he is responsible. It was very threatening."

"That's frightening," said Mayor Sydney. "Did he make any demands?"

Standing tall, Harry looked around, making eye contact with most of them. "Rolf has not made any specific demands yet. I am sure demands will be coming. This is big. I was afraid this would happen. The time has come to put every ounce of energy into ending this crisis."

A deputy from Bridgetown leaned in and asked, "Do you think Rolf is the one responsible for the others who are missing?"

Harry said, "Right now, I would say that's a strong possibility. We have to pull out all the stops to rescue them. I wish I could tell you more, but this is all I have for now."

Mayor Percy called out, "What do you need from me?"

"If you could work with the other mayors and form a central contact point at headquarters to coordinate all information, it would really help."

"You've got it, Sheriff. Go apprehend those thugs."

***

"We now know who we're looking for. They are devious and cunning. However, their smugness will be their downfall. Their carelessness is bound to leave some clues, and it's up to us to find them."

"You've got that right, Sheriff. I know first-hand about Rolf," said Stinky. "I still have nightmares of his darts being shot at me during the go-cart race."

Harry remembered and nodded to his friend. "I feel your pain."

"All right, Deputies. You all have your jetpacks. Strap them on. The first thing we'll do is a complete aerial survey over Pondville and all surrounding towns. Make sure you have your radios on so we can keep one another informed. Don't forget these."

Harry held up his Stun-erator. "And don't be afraid to use them. Remember, these culprits are going to throw everything they've got at us. It won't be nice. Be ready. Remember, we don't know where they are. They could pop out from anywhere. These kidnappers are dangerous hoodlums."

The deputies wasted no time putting their jetpacks on and holstering their Stun-erators.

Harry finished up. "I'm going to call up Captain Carl and his eagle squadron for support. They can fly up much higher than us. Their eyesight is so keen, they will be able to spot things we might miss. Okay, everybody, go out there and see what you can find. Meet back here in an hour to report in."

"Charlie, Wreck, you're with me."

\*\*\*

Unexpectedly, the trio heard a loud swoosh overhead. Captain Carl's squadron had arrived. They did a large flyby to check things out. This gave Captain Carl a good idea of how things stood before reporting in. They circled. Then Captain Carl swooped down and landed right next to Wreck. The eagle squadron hovered above, awaiting orders.

"Good afternoon. Right now, everything seems peaceful out there," reported Captain Carl. "You all look very concerned. What's up?"

Harry quickly said, "Sadly, I must tell you that Ludwig and Sally have been kidnapped by Rolf and his gang."

"No, not those two! I can't believe it. What do you want my squadron to do, Harry?"

"What I would like you to do is observe any unusual sightings or anything that doesn't seem right. My hope is that your squadron will find where Rolf and his cronies are hiding. You can fly higher than we can with our jetpacks, and your eagle eyes can see and pinpoint things much better than we can."

Captain Carl nodded. "That's something we can do, Sheriff. We'll head out and see what we can find and report back to you."

Following their captain, the eagle squadron zoomed straight up, leveled off about 200 feet in the air, and began their search.

*** 

Wreck rocked back and forth. "I am so worried about what those wolves will do to Sally and Ludwig.

They are my best friends. We have to save them. I don't know what I'll do if something happens to them."

"Don't worry, Wreck. Our deputies are the best. They are well trained. Let's get airborne and see what we can find."

"Yes, sir, Sheriff. Hop in. You too, Charlie. We'll nab those gangsters one way or another."

Harry warned him, "Keep an eye out for the deputies with jetpacks and for Earl the crow. He'll be flying where none of the rest of us can go. We don't want to hit any of our own. The last thing we need is a casualty."

Wreck said, "Will do."

"Charlie, keep an eye out for anything out of the normal."

"Copy that, Sheriff. I've got my binoculars right here to give me a closer look."

***

An hour later, they all met back at headquarters. One by one, each deputy stated that there was nothing new or unusual to report. Everything seemed normal and quiet.

"Come on, guys, there's something we're missing."

The deputies looked at one another. They had never heard Harry speak like this.

He kept tugging at the few strands of hair on his head. "There must be a clue somewhere. Let's get back out there and find it. Dismissed."

\*\*\*

The deputies returned to headquarters that evening. They had spent a grueling afternoon surveying Pondville and the surrounding towns, and still had nothing to report.

Captain Carl spoke up. "I would like to report something that seems suspicious. It needs to be checked out right away. My squadron detected a beaver dam way upstream, under the cover of thick vegetation."

Chief Deputy Bart asked, "How do you know it's a beaver dam? What's unusual about that?"

"Because of the tree stumps and chewed-up logs all around the area. A large pool of water has formed behind the dam, which prevents water from flowing to Pondville. That is what, I think, has caused a water shortage in the pond."

Harry said, "Great spotting. Maybe this is the break we were looking for."

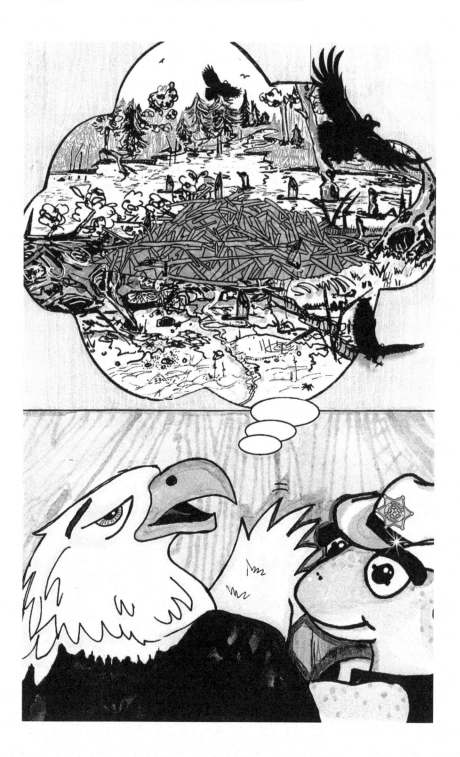

"Sheriff, I have an idea. My squadron and other eagle squadrons from all over the world take refresher courses on navigation and patrol techniques. This keeps our skills up to the highest level. Our latest course just ended. Two colleagues from the Yukon and the Northwest Territories are still in the area. Would you like me to ask them if they could help us out in our time of need?"

"Wow," said Harry, "that would be wonderful. The more help we can get, the better the chances of solving this. Go for it."

"On it."

Harry looked at everyone. "It's late now and getting dark. At daybreak we'll resume our patrols and a few of us will proceed to the dam for a closer look. Now, Earl, this is where you come in. You will fly in and out of the places where it would be impossible for the rest of us to go."

"Got it, Sheriff."

"Dismissed."

# Chapter 14

Sally and Ludwig sat chained to the floor of the dungeon. What a sorry sight they were!

Sally clanked her chains in an attempt to reach out to Ludwig. "How are you doing, Professor?"

"I'm fine, except for the fact that I am thirsty and hungry. How about you, Sally?"

"Okay, I guess ... under the circumstances."

"At least they took the gags out of our mouths."

"That smelly gag dried up my mouth, but I can handle it. We're not going to let those despicable hoodlums win this battle."

"I'm with you, Sally. We may look a mess right now, yet our spirits remain strong. My biggest fear has come true. I dreaded that X-rocks might fall into the wrong hands and it has happened. This could wreak havoc on our way of life in Pondville. There is no way they'll get the secret out of me. Not only that, but Harry also understands the power of X-rocks and he knows I would never give up the secret."

"I know, Ludwig. Your ethics are what I truly admire about you. We both know our sheriff. And we know he will do his best to find us and put an end to Rolf's despicable gang." Sally sighed and tried to get comfortable on the dungeon floor. It had been a very trying day. The chains and handcuffs kept getting in the way. *If only I could go to sleep. I need to rest. I'm so exhausted.*

*** 

Meanwhile, Thor went to the throne room to update Rolf. "They have an all-out alert to find us."

Rolf rubbed his big mangy paws together. "Three cheers for them. That's okay. This is what I expected. We'll be ready for them. Anyway, we have hostages. Those pond scums are so important to Pondville, Harry won't take a chance with their lives. That's our big advantage. We'll use Sally and Ludwig to prevent an all-out attack against us."

"You are so smart and cunning, Boss. The sheriff will be afraid for his little friends. He won't want them hurt, that's for sure."

"Imagine if Ludwig was badly hurt or killed," said Rolf. "Pondville would crumble without his immense contributions. And Sally is the organizer and glue that keeps the community working together harmoniously. Now, go to the dungeon and bring those two losers up here."

Rolf jumped out of his throne and said, "Oh, Thor, before you go. Get that big pot of water boiling. We'll terrify them by threatening to put them in the pot. When they hear the water bubbling and see the steam rising, it will scare the living daylights out of them, especially that sassy Sally."

Twenty minutes later, to the sound of chains clinking and dragging along the floor, the wolves escorted Sally and Ludwig to the throne room. The prisoners looked smug, but were a bit afraid. The noise from their chains intimidated them. They stood in front of Rolf.

Growling, Rolf looked each of them in the eye. "Keep your mouths shut and speak only when spoken to," he said. "Any outburst, a gag will be shoved back in your mouth to shut you up. Got it?"

Sally sneered and said, "You don't scare me."

"You want to test me?"

"No."

"Then shut up."

Rolf directed his attention to Ludwig. "Have you come to your senses, Professor? Are you ready to give us the information we want?"

Ludwig stood tall and said, "No matter what you do to me, I'll never tell."

"Bravo, Ludwig," said Sally.

"If I were you, Sally," said Rolf, smirking, "I'd try to convince him to tell us what he knows and to cooperate with us … for your sake."

"Do you really think I would try to convince him? Never in a million years would I do that."

Rolf pointed to the pot of boiling water to make sure his prisoners understood his terrifying plan. "You know," he said, "I am a softhearted guy. So I'm going to send you back to the dungeon to think it over. It would be wise on both your parts to do so."

Rolf waved to the guards. "Get 'em out of here. I can't stand the sight of those two."

After their trudge to the depths, they were again chained to the floor of the dungeon.

Sally asked Ludwig, "What do you think about Rolf's scare tactics?"

"He's a mad wolf and he'll do anything to get what he wants."

"I'll tell you, he scares me with that pot of boiling water," she said with a shudder. "I don't have any idea about how to convince him to change his mind. Do you?"

"No. It's obvious he has a mission and is determined to carry it out. He won't budge. All we can hope for is a daring rescue. I know our friends in Pondville will do all they can to free us. I hate to admit it, but it doesn't seem hopeful at this moment."

"I know what you mean." Feeling miserable, Sally was lost in thought. She reminisced about the past and how wonderful it was … the close friendships, play times, lunch by the pond, waterskiing, gondola rides, and, most of all, the derby … all so much fun.

Ludwig, on the other hand, recalled his inventions. He remembered how he created them, his go-cart adventures, the derby, Wreck's transplant, the jetpacks, and so much more. He was determined to hold fast and not give up any inventions related to the X-rocks. He pondered, *What a long night this will be for us.*

## Chapter 15

Just before dawn, everybody met at the sheriff's office.

"Today is critical to the happiness and peace of our region." Harry looked each deputy in the eye. "Are you with me?"

Every deputy nodded. Several said, "Copy that."

"I see we have some new members added to our search team," said Harry. "Captain Carl, please introduce them."

Captain Carl stood up with a proud look on his face. "I would like you to meet Captain Ron Jayhawk—known as Hawk—from the Yukon, and Captain Gilbert Snowbird—known as Blizzard—from the Northwest Territories. They refer to me as Captain Cool. As I mentioned before, they are the best."

"Welcome aboard," said Harry. "We can use all the help we can get."

Captains Hawk and Blizzard stepped forward, nodded, and gave each other a high five.

"Let me make a suggestion," Carl said. "Our squadrons can fly anywhere from 200 to 500 feet high. With the three squadrons, we can cover much more territory in a shorter time, then report our findings immediately. You will have the latest info to act on. Remember our squad spotted what looked like a beaver dam on our last flyby. Imagine, with two more squads we can cover triple the territory in the same amount of time."

"Fresh eyes and new ideas ... love it." Harry gave a thumbs-up.

Carl added, "There seems to be another large clump of something suspicious nearby. We couldn't make it out. We can check it by diving closer on this leg of our search." With a nod, he sat down.

"Are there any other suggestions or ideas?" The sheriff gazed around the room. "No? Then let's get ready to do everything in our power to find the kidnap victims."

No one spoke, waiting for the next words from Harry.

"Here is the plan. Charlie and I will start our search in Wreck, with Earl flying alongside. We'll go in solo when the terrain requires it." Harry was about to finish his instructions when Carl jumped in.

"One more suggestion. Why don't our squadrons leave right now and do another survey of the area. This way, we can give everybody a heads-up on the latest info before going in. Not only will we verify what we saw before, but who knows what more we will discover."

Harry rubbed his chin. "I'm okay with that. We will cool our heels and wait for your next report."

*** 

The eagle squadrons shot straight up, leaving a wind blast behind them. Everyone grabbed their hats so they wouldn't blow away.

Moments later the eagles settled at 350 feet, flying on cruise control. The landscape and sky were clear. This was business as usual for the eagles, and yet they couldn't help but admire the beauty of the greenery below.

Captain Carl spoke into his headset. "Hey, guys. We couldn't ask for better weather than this."

"Too bad we can't bottle this clear day," replied Hawk.

Blizzard chimed in, "The beauty of this day is the clarity."

Carl said, "Let's spread out and cover more territory."

"Roger that," all responded.

After several minutes, Hawk called out, "Drift over to my area. Something looks suspicious."

As they came closer together, they dropped down to about 200 feet and cruised along.

Hawk pointed, saying, "See that clump of trees? If you look beyond them, there is something large that looks like a castle."

"I can't ever recall anything like that being here," Carl pondered aloud.

*Whoosh!*

Blizzard exclaimed, "What was that!"

"I don't know," said Carl, "but whatever it was, I don't like it one bit."

*Whoosh!*

Carl said, "Yikes, that was close. Let's fly the coop before one of us is hit. The sheriff needs to hear what we've found."

\*\*\*

Twenty minutes went by as Harry and Charlie paced back and forth in the office. They could not stay still.

The squadrons returned.

Captain Carl could not wait to spill the goods. "Here's what we found. There's definitely a fortress and a dam. Be extremely careful going in. Our squadrons were attacked with airborne weapons when we dove down to recon. They looked like fiery arrows."

Blizzard said, "We hightailed it out of there as fast as we could."

Carl went on. "We never thought we would be shot at, and weren't prepared to protect ourselves. We'll know better next time and go in with shields. Those fiery arrows could really do a job on our tail feathers."

Blizzard and Hawk nodded in assent.

Harry paced, giving out orders. "Okay, listen up. Let's go over what I said before. Charlie and I will start our search in Wreck, with Earl flying alongside. We'll go in solo when the terrain requires it. The rest of you, don your jetpacks. Don't forget your Stun-erators and radios. Your task is to do a combination of land and aerial searching. Any other questions?"

Kim said, "Just one, Sheriff. If we see something unusual or find someone, do we call headquarters or you?"

"For now, call me."

\*\*\*

Wreck sat, ready and waiting, eager to move.

"Charlie," Harry said, "did you put our jetpacks in the rumble seat? I want to be ready to go solo if there are areas Wreck can't fit into."

Wreck said, "It will take a jungle to stop me from going in."

Harry thought, *That's my Wreck.* "Charlie, the jetpacks?"

"Done. I also put our Stun-erators in the front seat, along with the radios."

Harry and Charlie hopped into Wreck.

"Are we ready?"

Two yeses.

"Let's get airborne."

They could feel the heaviness of anticipation in the air as they took off on their mission.

Scouring the area, Harry spotted what might be a dam under thick vegetation. "Charlie, do you see what I see? Is that a dam?"

"Yeah, it looks like one to me."

"Wreck, I know you can't go in there. So fly over to the open field and let us out. Charlie and I will fly above the stream to see the lay of the land and the dam. Earl, you go into the areas thick with brush and take a good look."

Once Wreck landed, Charlie and Harry got out. They put on the jetpacks.

"Wreck, circle above. If it seems that we need reinforcements, it will be your job to go get them. Understand?"

"Sure do, Harry. I won't let you down. Be careful."

Harry gave Wreck a thumbs-up.

"Charlie, got everything?"

"Yup."

"Okay, let's go in."

***

Nearing the area with thick vegetation, Harry said in a low tone to Charlie, "Watch out. We have to be careful around here. We don't want to get hurt."

They wove in and out between the trees and bushes.

As they slowed down, Harry said, "There is something over there. Can you see it, Charlie?"

"Yeah, Captain Carl was right. It's a beaver dam."

"Let's move in a little closer."

Just then, Earl flew over to talk to Harry and Charlie. "Did you see the beaver dam?"

"Yes," said Harry.

As they approached the dam, Charlie spotted something more dramatic, more impressive, beyond the dam.

The crow yelled out, "Oh my gosh, what is that? It looks like a fortress."

"You're right," Harry said, "that's what it looks like. Let's move closer."

"It has a moat around it and there's a drawbridge," Charlie called out. "It seems like the only way in."

Out of nowhere, a fiery arrow zoomed right by them.

"What was that!"

"Let's get out of here now," said Harry. "I think we found their hideout."

*** 

Wreck was flying low over the treetops. A couple of arrows shot up from the trees and hit a side door.

"Ouch, ouch—that hurt. I'd better leave, fast."

Harry radioed to Wreck, "Let's go!"

Wreck squawked, "I know, I know."

"All right. Okay, Wreck. Head over to the place we landed before. Charlie, Earl, and I will meet you there."

"Roger that."

*** 

At the landing field, Harry asked Wreck, "Are you sure you're all right?"

"Yeah, I'm okay. I was hit by something hot. I think they were fiery arrows. Whatever, they sure didn't tickle."

"Over here." Charlie motioned to Harry. "A flaming arrow hit the back door and it's a little scorched ... nothing more than that. Are you sure you're all right, Wreck?"

Wreck's grill scowled. "You bet I am. That makes me really mad. I'm even more ready to go."

Harry explained. "From what I saw, the big stream that always fed the pond is almost completely shut off. The dam prevents the water from flowing down to the pond and causes a buildup of water that supports the moat. The chewed-up tree stumps confirm it's a beaver dam."

"What should we do?" asked Wreck.

Harry paused and gathered his thoughts. "We have to demolish the dam. That should start water flowing back down to Pondville. If we do it right, the moat will probably drain. That'll clear the way for us to attack."

"That doesn't sound easy, Harry."

"Yeah, Charlie, I agree. We have to try. I've got a feeling we can do it. Wreck, you and Earl head back to headquarters. Round up all the deputies you can muster. Fill them in on what's happening and send them to the dam site."

"Got it," said Wreck.

Earl signaled agreement.

"Meanwhile, Charlie and I will try to blast the dam by increasing the power of the Stun-erators and see what happens. Hopefully we can do it. One more thing. Sound the alert for a possible flash flood in Pondville. We don't want anyone needlessly hurt."

"We're on our way," Earl said. "Good luck trying to blast the dam."

# Chapter 16

Harry and Charlie flew to the beaver dam. Little did they know they had tripped an alarm alerting the fortress's guards. Soon, Harry and Charlie heard sirens blaring from the fortress.

"Darn, that settles that," grumbled Harry. "The sirens gave us away. They know we're here."

The two jetpacking frogs moved at high speed and landed on the same side of the dam to check it out.

Harry said, "Nobody is around. The beavers are probably inside their lodge resting. We'll each grab a tree branch. I'll pound the side of the dam and you pound the water. The noise may alert anybody who's inside."

As they pounded away, a beaver popped his head out and said, "What the heck is going on here?"

"I am Sheriff Harry, and I order you to vacate the premises. We are about to blow this dam apart."

"What? You can't do that. This is our family home. Besides, Rolf the wolf will be fuming and he'll have our heads. He's the one who forced us to build it. He ordered us to live here and guard the dam and his fortress. He let us know in no uncertain terms that it was in our best interest to obey him. We didn't dare say no. That wolf is a terror."

"Vacate immediately," Harry stated. "Don't worry about Rolf and his gang. We'll deal with them. I advise you to skedaddle out of here right now. We'll put you under our witness protection plan. Move out now." He gestured for them to move to high ground. "There are no ifs, ands, or buts about it."

The beaver ducked into the lodge. "Emma, Emma," he cried out, "where are you? Everybody out, everybody get out. They're about to blow this place apart!"

"For goodness' sake, what is it now, Clem? Can't you see I'm busy cleaning up your mess and all the woodchips you leave hanging around?" yelled Emma, hands on her hips.

"Listen. I'm not kidding. We must leave now. The sheriff and his deputies are about to blow this place apart!"

"Oh no!" cried Emma. "Just when I get this place homey looking and exactly the way I want it."

"Never mind that. Call Leroy and Grandpa Joe, and I'll alert the others to get out."

Emma ran back to Leroy's room and shouted, "Leroy, come out, we have to get out!"

"Mom, can't you see I am busy playing my game? You said if I cleaned my room, I could."

"I said now. Move it."

Emma called out, "Grandpa Joe, Grandpa Joe, where are you?"

"I'm in here, on my rocking chair, chewing on my corncob pipe. What is it?"

Emma scurried into his room. "Grandpa, hurry. We must evacuate. They are going to blow this place up."

Grandpa stopped rocking and said, "Why are they going to blow up our place? You've got to be kidding."

"No, I'm not. I don't know why. We must get out now and move away from the dam."

One by one, the members of the colony exited the dam. Charlie and Harry motioned for them to move quickly and gather on the side of the hill.

When he saw Harry, Grandpa Joe stopped. Leaning on his cane, he wagged his finger in Harry's face and said, "You know, Sheriff, it is very inconsiderate of you to cause this upheaval. I don't approve of this at all. You come along and destroy our happy lives."

Harry smiled at the elderly gent and said, "You'll understand later why this has to be done."

Hotfooting it up the hill, one beaver scowled and said, "After I set up good housekeeping, I have to move out. What a disgrace!"

Her friend replied, "I guess it's better than being blown up."

The beaver colony sat out of the way on a small mound, ready to watch the action. They couldn't believe it when they saw the two frogs flying around.

Charlie and Harry hovered slightly above, aimed their Stun-erators at the dam, and shot. Dirt and debris flew up and around, but the dam remained standing.

They tried again ... and again.

No results.

"Darn, this is not working," said Harry, throwing his arms up in exasperation. "There's not enough power to blow the dam apart."

Charlie said, "I see a small trickle of water has started flowing down to Pondville."

Harry noticed Wreck arriving with the troops, so he motioned to Charlie to come with him to meet them at the clearing.

Wreck called out, "I brought some sticks of dynamite, just in case."

"Fantastic," said Harry. "That should do it. Let me think for a minute." Harry paced around and scratched his head a few times before coming to a stop. "Here's the plan. Charlie and I will fly in and determine the best places to put the dynamite. We'll mark the areas. The idea is to blow up the dam without causing a major gusher. We'll do it area by area to prevent a flood. Let's call it a strategic drain. The rest of you should remain here until the dam is destroyed and the moat is drained."

Harry and Charlie flew back to the dam to give the beaver colony an update. "Attention, everybody! The deputies will maintain their positions at the clearing until the dam is blown."

"What about us?" asked one beaver.

Harry said, "You must move far enough away to protect yourselves. There'll be a lot of stuff flying around when the dam blows. To be safe, I suggest you go even higher up the hill."

Clem stepped forward and said, "Before we move away, would you like us to clear a small area so your car can get closer to the action?"

"That's a great idea," said Harry. "Thank you."

In no time, the beavers took down enough trees for Wreck to land closer. They also pulled the trees off to the side to create a small clearing.

Wreck said, "Thank you, guys. That was most kind of you."

\*\*\*

From the east tower, Rolf watched the beavers through his binoculars. "What are they doing taking down those trees?"

All of a sudden it hit him. "They're making a clearing. It can only be for that hateful sheriff and his car. Those beavers are traitors. A curse on them and their families. Oh, they are going to pay. No one betrays me and gets away with it. Blackie, add them to my *list*. Then bring Ludwig and Sally to the throne room."

***

The prisoners clanked into the throne room. They looked bedraggled, filthy, and dispirited. Rolf picked up on their feelings right away.

He bared his sharp teeth and said, "Have you come to your senses? Do you agree to give me what I want?"

In unison, they said, "No."

Both stood there steadfast. Though Ludwig was sweating, he acted cool and calm. Sally's eyes narrowed, sending a piercing stare at Rolf, as if looks could kill.

"Okay. No more Mr. Nice Guy! Blackie, remove Sally's chains and drop her in the pot of boiling water."

As soon as Blackie began to undo her chains, Ludwig screamed, "No, no, don't do that. Please, please. I'll tell you what you want to know." *Not my dearest friend Sally!*

She said, "Stop, Ludwig. Stand strong. You can't let everyone in Pondville down. You don't have to do this." Sally was terrified, shaking, yet still defiant.

"Yes, I do. I can't bear to let you suffer that way."

"If you give me what I want," Rolf said with a wink and a sly look, "both of you will be spared."

# Chapter 17

"Come gather around Wreck," Harry said to his deputies. He stood on the driver's seat for the best visibility. "We need to open a hole in the dam so we can drain the moat and allow a normal flow of water back to Pondville. We don't know what's in the moat. You can be sure that those shifty wolves put something in there that could hurt us."

Charlie said, "We know darn well the moat contains something dangerous. It could be anything. Remember how Rolf rigged his go-cart to shoot darts." Charlie shrugged his shoulders. "Who knows?"

"Yeah, I agree. All right now, I need six volunteers."

Ten arms went up within seconds.

"Thank you. The first six, stand over here by the dam. The other four, remain on standby in case we need you."

Harry pointed to the six deputies. "Each of you grab three sticks of dynamite and place them in the designated areas. Spacing is essential. Wait until I give you a signal to light the fuses. When I take my hat off and wave it, that will be your signal. Light the fuses and then get out of there *fast*. Got it?"

They nodded.

After the explosives were in place, Harry radioed headquarters. "Tell the deputies there to remain on standby in the event of a flood or any other emergency. Contact Dr. Bernie and let him know what's going on. Put him and his medical team on alert."

"Roger that, Sheriff."

"Everyone else, move back," yelled Harry. "I'm going to give the signal to light the fuses." He took his hat off and waved it.

Within seconds … *BAM, BAM, BAM, BAM, BAM, BAM!*

A good flow of water was pouring out down the hillside.

The beavers were cheering, yelling, "Awesome!" and "Fantastic!"

A few minutes later Harry radioed headquarters again. "How is the water flow coming along?"

"Pretty good, Sheriff. No damage so far," said the headquarters operator. "It is great to see the pond filling up and getting back to normal."

***

Just then Rolf heard some loud bangs. The flying debris from the explosions had activated the siren again.

Thor ran into the room, yelling, "We're about to be attacked!"

Rolf commanded, "Everyone to their defense positions. The time has come. This is our opportunity to wipe out all those losers."

One of the guards rushed Sally and Ludwig back to the dungeon.

Rolf's army was well trained. They ran up to the towers, taking their assigned positions. Rolf headed to the west tower with binoculars in hand. He couldn't wait to see his enemies destroyed.

Thor said, "Boss, the water in the moat is going down and it's almost empty. Our traps are exposed."

"I know, I know. Don't panic, Thor. That just means we'll have to rely more on our catapults along the upper wall. We have the advantage up here. We need to be accurate when we launch them.

Bring some more oil and soak the ammunition until it drips. The boulders and oil-soaked fireballs from the catapults will knock anything out of the sky. Keep a close lookout for any movement. Once we see any one of those flying deputies, we go into action."

***

Blackie returned Sally and Ludwig back to the dungeon. He ran out, not realizing he had dropped the keys for the chain locks.

Sally slid across the grimy dungeon floor and stretched out to grab the keys with her foot. She quickly unlocked their chains.

"Ludwig, I think the rescue team is out there. I bet our great sheriff is leading the attack on the fortress. I knew he would come to rescue us."

Ludwig's hopes soared. "We should stay put until the attack is over. I don't even want to think what Rolf would do if he saw us now. Besides, there is nothing we can do to help our rescue team."

"I agree. Our best bet is to remain here until we are rescued."

# Chapter 18

"Okay, deputies, here's the plan. Charlie will scout the area around the fortress and report back. Then we'll decide our next steps."

"Copy that, Sheriff." Charlie flew up about 10 feet and approached the fortress. A dozen flaming arrows flew at him. He easily dodged them while flying over the moat to scout the perimeter. Then he shot straight up another 30 feet to get a better look inside the fortress. More flaming arrows. *Boy, they're good. These guys are ready!*

No matter how many arrows they shot at him,
Charlie managed to stay out of harm's way.

Rolf yelled, "Come on, guys, you keep missing him.

We've got to knock that pesky tattooed frog out
of the sky. He can't be that good at dodging our
arrows." Rolf realized that the thing on Charlie's
back allowed him to react instantly.

Rolf stared, his lower jaw hanging open. He was
blown away by Charlie's maneuvers. He shouted,
"Get ready. This battle is going to be tougher than
I thought."

Charlie finished scouting and returned to report
his findings to Harry. "Here's the problem, Sheriff.
Their defense is well spread out. No matter what side
we attack, they'll meet us equally at every position. I
got a good look at the moat. It's completely drained.
There are leg traps and razor-sharp blades spread out
along the bottom. It would be treacherous to go in
on foot. And across the top of the fortress, there are
catapults loaded with boulders and fireballs. It's not
only the catapults. The wolves are also armed with
bows and arrows that have fiery tips—the same
kind they shot at Wreck. They can defend against
an aerial attack, and that is our only way in."

"Good job, Charlie. So, that limits our attack
plan," Harry said, rubbing his chin as he spoke.
"We have to attack by air. This is where the jetpacks
come in handy."

"You are so right, Sheriff. Thank goodness I had mine on," Charlie said with a sigh of relief. "They shot their arrows at me, but I managed to dodge them. Phew!"

"Deputies, this is what I propose," Harry said. "We will attack the south side of the fortress. Leave plenty of room between each other. The key to success is our ability to weave in and out and stay clear of their firepower. We need to fly out of range of the catapults until their ammo is gone, and then fly in, dodging the arrows. Using our Stun-erators, we can overtake them. Let's move 10 feet apart and stay in formation. We don't want to be easy targets."

\*\*\*

From the hillside, Clem called out, "Good luck, you guys. May the power be with you. Knock 'em out."

Leaning over, another beaver whispered, "This is going to be some battle. My money is on the sheriff and his deputies."

\*\*\*

The deputies prepared for orders to attack.

Harry pumped his fist up and down twice and shouted his commands: "Onward and upward. Fly above the catapults' range and prepare to dodge their arrows."

Seeing the deputies coming, Rolf instructed his gang: "When they get close enough, release the catapults."

The battle began. Catapults shot out hot boulders. Every boulder whizzed below the intended targets. Harry and the deputies dodged the firepower until Rolf exhausted his first line of defense.

Harry glanced at Charlie and said, "Phew, they missed us! It's obvious our training has paid off."

Rolf's next line of defense was shooting fiery arrows. At his command post, Rolf yelled, "Shoot 'em. Knock 'em out of the sky. Don't let those lowlifes get near us."

Harry called out to his deputies, "Fire your Stun-erators whenever they are reloading."

As the wolves prepared their arrows, the deputies reacted by firing the Stun-erators at them. One by one, Rolf's hoodlums were taken down. Within no time, Rolf's defense gang was immobilized; they were lying there, unable to move. The deputies quickly landed and zip-tied them all to prevent escape. A few had to be re-stunned.

Harry and Charlie descended to the south tower and raced inside the fortress to look for the captives. When Ludwig and Sally heard the commotion, they ran out of the dungeon and into a narrow hallway. They could hear Harry and Charlie calling out their names.

"We are down here," yelled Ludwig.

Charlie had opened the heavy outer door of the dungeon.

Sally ran up the steps and threw her arms around Charlie and Harry. Tears streamed down her face. "Thank you, thank you. Rolf was going to kill us if Ludwig didn't give up the secret info of the X-rocks."

"Professor, what a delight to see you," Harry said, beaming. "I was really worried I might not get a chance to beat you in the next derby race."

Ludwig looked at Harry, winked, and said, "Yeah, right!"

Charlie patted Ludwig on the back.

\*\*\*

After the prisoners were secured, several of the deputies gathered in the throne room to report to Harry.

Chief Deputy Arthur stepped forward. "Sheriff, Rolf and three of his closest confidants are nowhere to be found. Apparently, they escaped somehow."

Harry said, "Clinger, put a team together and do one last search."

Twenty minutes later they reported back. "Nothing, Sheriff, but we did find a tunnel that leads out of the fortress."

"Clinger, go outside with a few deputies and scour the area to see if you can locate them."

"On it, Sheriff," said Clinger.

"Arthur, Stinky, and Jake, gather the prisoners and march them to the Pondville jail."

Arthur asked, "How do you want us to handle the kidnapped wolf pups?"

"Put them with the other kidnap victims. Bart and Kim will deal with them later."

All the kidnap victims had been accounted for. Most were in bad shape, yet thrilled to be going home. The wolf pups had a different attitude. Most had become mini thugs and gang members under Rolf's training. Some work was going to be needed to reintroduce them to normal community life.

"Bart and Kim, see to the captives and bring them home. If they need any medical attention, take them to Pondville General. The wolf pups may give you trouble. If so, separate the ones who think they are gang members and keep them in the holding tank. We'll deal with them later."

"Okay," said Bart.

"Meanwhile, Wreck, Charlie, and I will take Ludwig and Sally to the hospital to be checked out by Dr. Bernie."

# Chapter 19

Two days later, Harry held a press conference. It was open to anybody who lived in the region. Everyone was eager to hear about the successful raid on the fortress and the return of the captives.

Harry stood at the podium, flanked by his deputies.

"This meeting will now come to order," he said.

"I'm here to give you an update. First, all residents who were kidnapped have been accounted for. They were checked out at Pondville General Hospital and all were discharged. The last time I saw any of them, they were eating up a storm." Harry grinned.

A large round of applause broke out.

Harry continued. "The attack on Rolf's fortress was successful because of our dedicated deputies and their new equipment invented by Professor Ludwig."

There was a standing ovation and several shouts of "Hear, hear!"

"Ludwig and Sally have each been given a clean bill of health. They have resumed their normal activities," Harry said. "The young wolf cubs that were forced to become members of the wolf pack will be going to rehab facilities. Many were brainwashed and didn't know any better than to do as Rolf and his gang told them. No charges will be brought against them. The cubs will be on probation for six months. The Good Citizens Chapter, headed by Jake and Clinger, will monitor them. If no problems arise, their records will be cleared. I don't foresee any problems."

More applause.

Mayor Percy asked, "What about Rolf?"

"I am sorry to report that he and three of his leaders escaped during the raid. We have not stopped looking for them."

"He always was a sneaky wolf," said Mayor Sydney. "I'll bet he had an escape plan right from the start."

"Let's move on to the topic of the pond's water level," said Harry.

"Thanks go to Captain Carl. He was the first to discover that beavers had dammed the stream. As you can see, we took care of that and the pond is full.

"I would like to acknowledge the help of the two squadrons from the Northwest Territories and the Yukon. No question that without their help, things would have been a lot tougher. Right now they are headed back home. Please stand, Captain Carl."

He stood and acknowledged everyone with a smile and a wave. The crowd gave a loud round of applause. Many cheered and whistled.

"Carl, please offer my deep appreciation to "Will gladly do so, Sheriff."

"And now an update on the beaver colony. They

are without a home. We will help them relocate. They were terrified of Rolf and did his bidding. They are our friends. They know better now than to dam any streams that feed our pond."

A few laughs rose from the crowd.

"We have ordered a huge safe that will be under Professor Ludwig's control in his lab. It is critical to ensure the safety of our power supply. Our new high-powered equipment will be under lock and key in a new security room that Charlie is building at the Sheriff's Department. Our goal is to make sure it never falls into the wrong hands.

"Kim and Arthur have reported that our deputies learned a lot of new procedures which will help the PBI become a very strong investigative team. And I'll say it again ... we could not have done this without Ludwig's inventions."

More applause.

"Last but not least, we have no clue where Rolf, Thor, Joey, and Blackie are hiding. Looking forward, this means we must be diligent in watching for any threats from Rolf or any of his gang members. You never know."

The crowd seemed shocked by this news about

Rolf. Just when they thought things would be fine, another black cloud loomed over them.

"That's all I have for today, folks. Stay safe. Remember, Pondville's finest are looking out for you." With a touch to the brim of his sheriff's hat, Harry closed the meeting.

\*\*\*

"Can you believe those slimy, lowlife losers put up this poster?" Rolf spurted out to his partners in crime. "They will never catch us!"

*What does this mean for Pondville's future?*

*Are the citizens actually safe?*
*Does this mean they must always be on guard?*

**Stay tuned for Book 5!**

# Dr. Bob's Tales

## The End

Look for Harry and his friends' next adventure,
and visit us at: DrBobsTales.com.

## About Dr. Bob's Tales

Dr. Bob's Tales were inspired by my imagining different characters living around a pond. The pond became the centerpiece for the town of Pondville. Pondville turned into a community populated by diverse, relatable, and memorable characters, many of them loveable. The main cast of characters appears in every book. New ones are introduced as the plots unfold in each book. Lessons are taught subliminally. The culture of Pondville is a lesson in itself.

Readers get to know the characters and follow their exploits. For some readers, the Pondville characters become lasting imaginary friendships.

It is through discussing the stories with friends, family, in school, or in book groups that the lessons really pop.

No one can forget the 15th Annual Go-cart Derby in Book 1, *Hurry-Up Harry*, when Harry, Ludwig, Rolf, Stinky, and Charlie speed around the racetrack. It's great to see who has sportsmanship, who doesn't, and who shows up as the winner. Many readers can see themselves through the participants' eyes. Stinky just wants to race and have a good time. Rolf wants to win at all costs, even if he hurts someone else. Who will win?

Book 2, *Harry and the Hooligans*, throws out a challenge to the town and its good citizens. We see Harry maturing and taking over as the sheriff. He forms a wild and wily posse, and they form a plan to catch the hooligans who are robbing the general store. The story is action packed, and shows how "going along to get along" can lead to bad consequences. And, can the hooligans make up for their wrongs?

Book 3, *Harry Saves Wreck*, shows how the leaders in the town and the residents come together to save Wreck, the old sheriff's car. What actions do the Pondville residents take to express how they love and value him?

Book 4, *Harry and the Kidnappers*

Book 5 is on the way!

Please enjoy the discussion guide, or create your own.

Dr. Bob

## Discussion Guide

1. Since his go-cart racing days, Harry has matured quite a bit. After becoming sheriff of Pondville, he dealt with a robbery, a dilapidated sheriff's car, and now, kidnappers and a pond drying up. What changes do you see in Harry? How does he deal with the threat to his beloved friends and to Pondville?

2. Wreck is not just a car. He is an honorary deputy of the Pondville Sheriff's Department. What do you find amusing about Wreck when he tries anything new? Talk about his personality and his friendship with Harry.

3. Captain Carl is a take-charge eagle. What about him stirred your imagination?

4. Rolf is the classic bad wolf. Describe the way he behaves. What do you think makes him the way he is? Does he have some good characteristics? Can you name one or more?

5. Ludwig is a brilliant, creative turtle. How does he come up with ideas for his inventions? What do you like about Ludwig?

6. Rolf made scary threats to Sally and Ludwig. How did they deal with Rolf's threats?

7. Tilly, a bear, and Ludwig are a good team. They are different in so many ways. How are they different? What do you think is the secret to their teamwork? Would you want to be his apprentice? Why?

8. The sheriff's deputies worked well together to save Rolf's victims. What do you think made them work well together?

9. There are some funny scenes in this tale. Pick out your favorite. Describe it.

10. There are also some touching scenes in the story. Describe one or more. What did you feel?

11. If you could have one friend from this tale, who would it be? Why?

12. What is one lesson that you took away from *Harry and the Kidnappers*? How will you apply that lesson?

13. What do you think might happen in the next tale? What story do you think Dr. Bob might tell in Book 5?

## ABOUT THE POND

Foxhill Acres, my former home in Marriotts Cove, Nova Scotia, is a beautiful natural setting and provided me with inspiration. It is home to many of the indigenous creatures upon which my story characters are based. The idea for Harry started when a child heard the frogs croaking in the pond, and asked me, "Why?"

## Acknowledgments

### With special thanks to the following:

Frances Keiser, my guide, mentor, and designer who started the journey with me. She has always been there with support, encouragement, and information.

Beth Mansbridge, my copyeditor who went above and beyond the usual copyediting.

Rose E. Grier Evans, my illustrator who worked tirelessly to create the right illustration each and every time. She collaborated to the nth degree and always with a smile and words of encouragement.

Emily Coker, Cindy Dalecki, and Chris Gibson, my reviewers who gave of their time and provided valuable insights and feedback.

Ann Ernst, my partner in every sense of the word, who encouraged, collaborated, and challenged me as I wrote my fourth book.

## ABOUT THE ILLUSTRATOR

**Rose E. Grier Evans** is an award-winning book illustrator and has been a professional artist for more than thirty years. She was delighted to work with the author again, portraying his vision for *Harry and the Kidnappers*, and illustrating his story with whimsical details.

When not working on art projects, Rose is advocating for children or busy tending the goats on the family farm. She lives in North Central Florida with her husband, and enjoys spending time with their two grandchildren and other family members.

## About the Author

**Dr. Robert A. Ernst** is a retired orthodontist who practiced in central Connecticut for more than forty years. His education was interrupted when he joined the Air Force. He became a 1st lieutenant during the Vietnam era, before resuming his educational goals.

His early career as an author began in the form of a storyteller. Known as Dr. Bob, he created tales about the animals that lived around the pond at Foxhill Acres, his former home in Nova Scotia, Canada. He delighted neighboring children with the stories. In more recent years, his wife Ann convinced him to write down the stories in a series of books, and Dr. Bob's Pondville was created.

More tales are on the way from this award-winning author.

Dr. Bob and Ann reside in Florida.